Slam Dunks Not Allowed!

Dan Bylsma

&

Jay M. Bylsma

River Road Publications, Inc.

Spring Lake, Michigan

Hardcover ISBN: 0-938682-72-5
Paperback ISBN 0-938682-77-6
Printed in the United States of America

Library of Congress Control Number: 2002094922

Contents

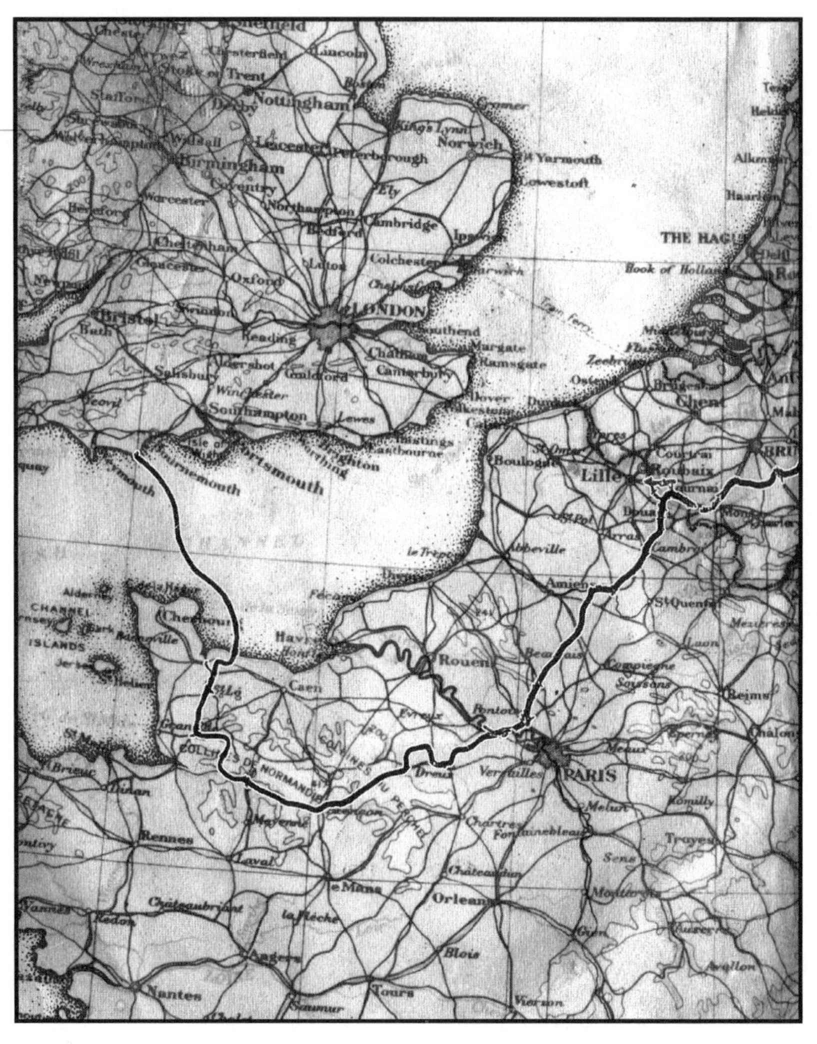

Grandfather Secory's Map

Chapter 1

A Letter from Germany

15 July 1944

Meine kostbarst Kinder:

Dieser sind schlechte Zeiten...hard times indeed. There is very severe rationing everywhere and we have not seen a shred of fresh meat or fruit in several weeks. God save us, we are virtually limited to what we can scratch from the miserable soil in our backyard or trade with our neighbors. You can barter a chicken for a winter coat... if you have a chicken or a winter coat.

That is not the worst of it, however. We have just received a whispered word sent from our cousin Rabbi Mendle that his brother—your cousin Jakob—and his family as well as all of our people in the town of Drent in the Netherlands have been taken from their homes and sent to camps where they are forced to work for the Nazi war effort. His son Yosef, may he rest in peace, was shot before his father's eyes for refusing to go. These Nazis are worse than animals. When we ask, what help can old women and children give the Nazis, we shake with fear. Perhaps the horrible rumors of death camps are true and we shall never see our relatives again.

We resolve not so say Kaddish *for them in the hopes the rumors are unfounded. There will be time enough for that when the time comes..."*

Isaac Greenberg stopped reading the letter from his father. His chest had become tight, and he could hardly catch his breath. He removed his glasses to wipe his eyes. The Greenbergs were gathered around the dining room table. The silence started in the corners of the room and quickly spread like a fog. They waited for him to compose himself and continue. But the only sound was the ticking of the clock on the china cabinet.

The ticking of the clock took young Samuel back to happier times. He often stopped by his grandfather's clock shop in Berlin where dozens of clocks would be ticking away. It was strange how standing in the middle of all those ticking clocks seemed to make time stand still. Just like now. Time seemed to stand still as Samuel listened to the clock and waited for his father to finish reading the letter.

The letter had arrived that day, bringing long awaited news from Samuel's grandfather and grandmother. They had remained in Germany when their son Isaac Greenberg took his wife and son and fled to America. Samuel remembered it well. They had settled in Grand Harbor, Michigan, with little more than the clothes on their backs in 1936 when he was ten years old.

Because of the war that raged in Europe, it was now impossible for the Greenbergs' relatives to leave. Mr. Greenberg's mother and father, as well as much of his extended family, were trapped in Germany, the Netherlands, Austria, and Poland. As Jews under the control of the Nazis, they were forced to wear bright yellow six-pointed stars on their coats when they went out in public. Some had their bank accounts frozen and then confiscated by the Nazis. Many of them were taken from their homes for "resettlement," never to be heard from again. The Greenbergs hadn't heard from Mrs. Greenberg's family for over two years. They hoped it was because no mail was getting out of Germany.

Samuel's father composed himself and began reading again.

You were right to go to America. You may be the lucky ones after all. We pray daily that the Allies will prevail against this horrible monster Hitler and soon. However, all the news here is that the Allied armies are being defeated at every turn.

If you would be so kind, please send canned meat. Who would have thought canned meat would be a gourmet treat and that we would be begging you for some? I trust you have enough to share.

And how is young Samuel? I expect he does well in his schooling and has kept up with his Hebrew lessons.

Enough already. My hands need to be coaxed to write these days, and making timepieces—once the joy and pride of my life—grows ever more difficult as the arthritis grows ever worse. To say the least, my heart is not in my work. Mama says I shouldn't complain; we have body and soul together. As my grandfather used to say, "It's not so bad to lose your teeth if there is no food."

May the God of Israel continue to keep us all in His hands. Shalom.

"How does *Grossvater* get these letters out of Germany, Papa?" Samuel asked.

"This one is postmarked from the Netherlands. God only knows how he gets them to the Netherlands. By way of his connections in the clock repair trade is my guess," Mr. Greenberg speculated. Then he paused and stared at the letter in front of him. Suddenly he looked up.

"*Lieber Gott!* If we read between the lines, I think there is a message here. He says, making timepieces. My father never made watches, or clocks for that matter. And he never called them timepieces. And later on he says his heart is not in his work. He always loved his work. I suspect we may have just learned why he has been spared and not sent off to the death camps."

"What do you think he is doing?" Aunt Nettie asked quietly.

"Making timepieces—timing devices for the Nazis," Mr. Greenberg answered.

"What do they do with timing devices?" Samuel wondered out loud.

"Bombs," was the soft answer.

"Grandpapa is working for the Nazis?" Samuel asked incredulously. "I don't believe it!"

"Not because he wants to, we can be sure of that."

The little group sat silently in stunned disbelief, contemplating what Mr. Greenberg had said.

"May I be excused? I need to do a homework assignment with Scooter." Samuel wanted an excuse to escape.

"You're excused, but don't stay too late. You have school tomorrow and basketball tryouts. You need your rest," Samuel's mother chided.

After the bustle of Samuel's departure, the silence crept in again. It was Samuel's aunt, Nettie Abrams, the schoolteacher with whom the Greenbergs had lived since they fled Germany, who finally broke the silence in her soft voice.

"I don't think our father would make bombs for the Nazis. I think he is cracking under the strain of the conditions there. There isn't anything we can do, that I can see. We must leave it in God's hands..."

"Leave it in God's hands?" Isaac Greenberg interrupted in a rage. "What God? Where is God? Do you see God in this letter? Where was God when they forced us to run like rabbits with nothing but the clothes on our backs? These animals would shoot a young man in cold blood before his father's eyes. Where was God then? Does he wait to save our people until they get to the door of the death camps?"

When he finished, he wiped the spittle from his lips. This time the silence was so thick that even the pendulum on the ticking clock seemed to slow down. Finally, Aunt Nettie spoke in her quiet way.

"They obviously haven't received any of our mail or they would know the Allies landed in France in June. It's now the first of November, this was written in July. We can only wait and hope the Allies win the war before..."

She couldn't bring herself to finish the sentence, and when she paused, Isaac Greenberg broke down and wept.

*****

Samuel hadn't bothered to put on a jacket since

Scooter lived only one house down and across Fourth Street. The early November air had a cold bite to it. He shivered and wondered if it was from the cold or the letter he had just heard read. His long legs allowed him to spring up onto the porch in one bounce, and he rang the bell.

It was a moment before the porch light came on and the curtains in the door parted. It was Merrill Secory, Scooter's aging grandfather, who was peering out to see who had interrupted his crossword puzzle. The door opened wide immediately.

"Samuel, Samuel, nice to see you. Calling for Scooter, are you? Well, come out of the night air or you'll catch your death of cold. And you without a jacket. What will become of our basketball team if our star center is down with a cold or worse?" The old gentleman closed the door, turned to face the stairs, and called, "Scooter! Scooter? There's a tall drink of water here to see you." And without waiting for Scooter to acknowledge his call, the old man turned back to Samuel.

"You know, Samuel, perhaps these old reading glasses are fooling me but I swear you're taller every time I see you. How tall are you there on the top end? Six-foot-three? Four?"

"Six-five, Mr. Secory."

"Six-five, eh? Maybe these olds specs aren't fooling

me after all. Can you reach the rim yet?"

Just then Gregory "Scooter" Secory came bounding down the steps. "Hi, Bergie. Come to work on the physics project?"

"Came to get out of the house, mostly. We got a letter from my grandparents."

"Really?" the old man asked. "Isn't that good news?"

"Not necessarily. It was written in July, and they say that my father's cousins in the Netherlands have been taken away. They shot my cousin Joseph."

"I'm so sorry to hear that. It's terrible what's going on over there. But at least you know that your grandparents were alive and well in July. That's better than no news at all."

"I suppose. Have you heard from your Uncle Rich?" Samuel asked turning to Scooter.

"No. Not for two weeks now. Last we knew he was still in France about a hundred miles from the German border."

The looks and the silence that followed told the story. The waiting was the worst. It filled the silences that occurred more often in a day than one would have guessed, particularly for Grandfather Secory. But even Samuel and Scooter, whose lives were busier, understood that everyone was waiting—waiting for word, any word, and hoping it wouldn't be the loss of a loved one.

Grandfather Secory broke the silence. "You best be at your project. What are the two of you rascals up to this time?"

"We're making a static electricity machine. It's a contest in physics class to see who can create the most static and generate the longest spark."

The old man peered over his glasses. "If you two don't win, I'll be shocked."

"If you want to be shocked, we'll let you hold the wire leads," Scooter said over his shoulder as the two high school seniors climbed the stairs to Scooter's room.

When Scooter's door closed, the living room settled into silence. This living room wasn't filled with worry about Jewish parents existing as outcasts in Berlin, but about a 19-year-old tech sergeant, a radioman in the Third Army that was presently in France fighting its way to the German border.

Merrill Secory was thinking about Rich Nagtzaam. Richie had become a part of the Secory family when he married Scooter's mother's youngest sister, Winifred. Like so many young men at the height of the war that was to become known as World War II, or W. W. Two, he had enlisted the day he graduated from high school.

Merrill remembered the day Richie and nearly 20 other young men—boys, really—gathered at the Pere Marquette train station in Grand Harbor to leave for their induction into the Armed Forces of the United States. They were a group filled with patriotic fervor and the braggadocio of youth, certain they could win the war for God and country. They would rid the earth of the Nazi hordes in Europe and the Japanese scourge in the South Pacific.

Their parents and sweethearts were there as well, but with quite different feelings. The more realistic among them knew that these would-be soldiers were little more than children, some of whom would never see the train station in Grand Harbor again. Parents and sweethearts might have to visit them in cemeteries filled with white crosses in the fields of Normandy or Iwo Jima or other places with strange sounding names, like Bastogne or Mindanao. Some would die as marines, some as fighter pilots, some as tank drivers, some as cooks.

Merrill Secory sighed as he remembered. The Secory family's last letter from Richie had been two weeks ago. At that time he was on the front lines (and sometimes behind the German lines) operating a radio or a telephone that communicated the conditions at the front and enemy troop movements to command posts. He also conveyed orders from the command posts to the soldiers in the front lines. All in all, it was perhaps as dangerous a job as there was in battle. From the newspaper accounts, it was clear that the fighting was fierce in the part of France where Richie was soldiering. Merrill Secory got up to turn the radio on to find something to drown out the silence and hurry the waiting. He found "The Jack Benny Comedy Hour."

In an upstairs bedroom, Scooter and Bergie (as Samuel Greenberg had come to be called by his friends) were busy poring over sketches of static electricity machines. Pictures of Leyden jars and prints of other devices whose counter-rotational moving parts generated static electricity, as well as rules (you could only use things commonly found around the house and garage) and hints, were spread on the desk and bed. However, the boys' topic of conversation was not electricity, but basketball.

Basketball tryouts for the Grand Harbor Pirates were scheduled for the next night, and the boys were filled with the hopes and fears that go along with such momentous events. Tonight they were filled with speculation: Who would make the team? Who would be disappointed?

"You're a shoo-in for center. Dutchie and Doolie are forwards for sure. Westie and Marv will make it. Then I have Jacob Merrill, Bub, Chappie and me for guards. Those guy's gotta make it. They were on varsity last year."

"I guess . . ." was all Bergie had to say.

"Some of 'em didn't play much, though. What about Woody? He's such a great guy and a real student of the game. He knows more about basketball than any two guys."

"I don't know . . ."

"I hope he makes it, just because he's so much fun to be around. But he's so small. I know he wants to make it real bad. I just don't think he's good enough and with his size. . . . You know, you don't make the team on smarts."

Scooter looked up from the pad he was scribbling names on. "What's the matter? You haven't said two words since you got here."

"Nothing."

Scooter wasn't convinced. "Is it your grandparents?"

Bergie shrugged and looked away. He looked like he had seen a ghost.

"Do you think they're dead?"

Bergie took a deep breath. "Can you keep this to yourself?"

"Sure. What is it?"

"We think my grandfather is making timing devices for bombs."

"Working for the Nazis? But isn't he . . . ? I mean, aren't they . . . ?"

"Jewish? Of course. Before this we couldn't figure out why they hadn't 'disappeared' like all of our other relatives that didn't get out of Germany before the war. But now my father thinks it's because they need his skills as a watch maker."

Scooter just looked at his tall friend.

"You think I'm a traitor or something?" asked Bergie.

"I don't think that and neither would anyone else. Everybody knows you got out to escape Hitler. Why would anyone think you were a traitor?"

"I don't know. I think every time I read about V-bombs, I'll wonder if my grandfather is making those things possible. Won't everyone else, too?"

"Do you know that for sure? Did he say that in the letter?" asked Scooter.

"No, but it's got to be that or something like that. Otherwise, why is he still alive and living in Berlin? A Jew?"

The boys were silent. Sounds from the radio in the living room seeped though the floor and around the cracks in the door.

Feeling responsible for the melancholy in the room, Bergie changed the subject. "Have you heard about cheerleading tryouts this afternoon?"

"Casey made it." Scooter said it as casually as he could, trying to hide his pleasure that his girlfriend had been selected.

"Oh ho! The captain of the basketball team and pretty cheerleader make all-American couple. I can see the headlines in the school paper now," Bergie said. He ducked as Scooter's pillow came hurling through the air.

"Who says I'll be captain? You? A lot you know. I think you've grown so tall you've outgrown your common sense, if not your brain. How's the weather up there, anyway?"

The pillow came flinging back at Scooter. "It'll be either you or Dutchie, although I can't see why. Neither of you have the sense to come in out of the rain. What a girl like Casey sees in you is beyond me." At that point the pillow made a return trip toward Bergie's head.

"Casey's a quality girl. If you would have paid attention in physics class, you would remember that liquids seek their own level, and this is a case of the cream rising to the top. What'd you get on the physics test on liquids, big boy?"

"An A."

"You cheat off'n Deloris TenBrink's paper?" Scooter asked, prompting the pillow to come back full force.

"I could have passed that test in three languages, which is more than I can say for some people I know. I wouldn't mention any names, of course, but his initials are Gregory Secory."

The banter and the speculation continued until the imaginary basketball team was settled on and Bergie left to go home. Both the boys fell asleep speculating, wondering, and hoping. For Scooter, the night's thoughts were pleasant, filled with the images of a cheerleader named Casey. Bergie's, however, were far more grim. What terror would force his beloved grandfather to work for the Nazis?

Chapter 2

Somewhere in the ETO

November 1, 1944
Somewhere in the European Theater of Operations

To my darling wife:

You can't believe the mud. It has rained heavily for more days than I can count, and the movement of men and vehicles has turned the roads into a quagmire. Nothing is clean, and there is no clean water anywhere. I am among the first Americans into an area and have seen horses of the retreating Germans dying on their feet because of exhaustion. They don't have the strength to pick their hooves up out of the thick mud. Funny how you feel sorry for a dead horse and not for its dead rider wearing a Nazi uniform.

Someone said there are 48 German horses and well over 50 French cows that died from the mud in this region alone. The local French farmers are butchering these carcasses for the meat. Sometimes I wonder what's more likely to send me to a field hospital, a German bullet or trench foot.

Somewhere in the ETO

I miss you so very much. This is a horrible war—too horrible to put into words. It is the memory of you, my dearest, and of my family and knowing that you pray daily for my safety that gives me the strength to carry on under unspeakable conditions. God bless you and keep me until we meet again. I love you so very much, my heart bursts to think of you.

Rich

P.S. Please call Charlie McKinney's family and tell them his wound was little more than a scratch. Their number is 6072 in Grand Rapids. It will also be his father's birthday end of this month. He'll be 51. Relay birthday greetings as Mac won't be doing any writing in the near future.

The letter had come in the morning mail and Scooter was eating lunch as he read it. "Have you figured out where he is, Gramps?" Scooter asked. His grandfather was poring over a large map of Europe. "He says 48 horses and 50 cows."

"What's horses and cows got to do with where he is?" Russell wanted to know.

Scooter looked at his eight-year-old brother, then at his mother. "If you know how many horses and cows there are in an area, you can tell where he is," Scooter lied. His mother kept on eating her soup as if nothing unusual had happened.

"I think he's near a town called Chaumont on the Marne River in the western part of France," Grandpa said as he returned to his place at the table. "That's a place in France where they have a lot of horses and cows, Russell."

"Is that up front?" Russell wanted to know.

"You mean the front lines," his grandfather corrected. "Yes, my boy, I'm afraid it is. No cushy desk job for your Uncle Rich. It sounds like he's seeing the war up close."

"Are we winning yet, Gramps?" Russell asked.

"From what I read in the papers, it looks like the Germans are retreating, and that confirms what your Uncle Rich says in his letter."

"What's trench foot?" Russell was full of questions.

"If your feet are exposed to cold and dampness for long periods of time, they begin to decay. Some of our soldiers haven't had a chance to change their socks for a long time, and they've been slogging about in mud, so their feet begin to rot."

"E-uuuew," Russell wrinkled up his nose at the thought.

"It looks like you've finished your soup. Take an apple to eat on the way back to school. Don't forget your rubbers, it's suppose to rain or snow this afternoon," their mother warned.

There was silence around the table after the back door closed, signaling Russell had started back to school. Scooter broke it. "I'm sorry, I wasn't thinking."

"I don't think there was any harm done, this time," his grandfather said. "But you never know who says what to whom and it's best we keep our little secret to ourselves if we want to continue to follow Rich's progress. I see we're finished. Why don't we let your mother clean up and you check my calculations."

When they were in the dining room, Scooter went to the large map of France spread on the dining room table. It had an irregular red line connecting red dots that had been positioned on the map. The dots represented the locations in which Uncle Rich had been. The connecting red line traced the path the Third Army had followed from Normandy on the western coast of France, through central France, through Paris, and toward the German border.

Scooter took a yardstick that was on the table and scanned the map. "Let's see, the first numbers mean where he was when he wrote the letter. He said 48 horses first—that means the 48th parallel." Scooter looked on the edges of the map and found the horizontal lines called latitude that divided the map into sections running from east to west. He found the line designated as the 48th. He noticed the 49th parallel ran right through Paris; the 48th was lower. He laid the yardstick along the 48th parallel.

"Then he said 50 cows, right?"

"Right."

Scooter then found vertical lines on the map. They ran from top to bottom and were called longitude lines. He found the line designated as 5. He knew that 50 really meant 5 point something, in this case 5.0. Scooter stretched a string from the top of the map to the bottom at the 5th longitude line. The edge of the yardstick and the string intersected exactly at a French town named Chaumont.

"How do you pronounce that, Gramps?" asked Scooter.

"I think that's pronounced sho-MOAN. When the Third Army gets into Germany, I can help you with the pronunciations, but my French is a bit rusty. You want to put a dot on the map and draw the route?"

Scooter did.

The map and the irregular line on it was the idea of Merrill Secory. Every letter from a soldier, even if sent from within the States, was read by military censors before being sent on to its destination. Any reference to the soldier's location or unit or his duty was blackened or cut out of the letters. Grandfather Secory's system that he worked out with Rich before he left—using latitude and longitude lines in code to communicate his location—was very much against the rules. Yet knowing the whereabouts of a son or husband was important information to the waiting families. If they could coordinate their soldier's movement with radio and newspaper reports, they knew if he was in the thick of the fighting or out of harm's way.

"Can you figure out where he's headed?" Scooter's grandfather asked.

"Let's see, you subtract two from each number in any telephone number for the latitude. He said the phone number was 6072, so that means he wants us to look at 4850," Scooter said, taking two away from each of the digits in McKinney's phone number. He put the yardstick on the map half way between the 48th and the 49th parallel. "Mr. McKinney's age is 51, so that would be 5.1." Scooter stretched the string along lines on the map that would indicate a longitude of 5.1. The string intersected the yardstick near a town named Metz. "So he's headed toward Metz," Scooter concluded.

Grandfather unfolded the *Grand Harbor Tribune* from the night before. The headline read "Third Army Molds Arc Around Metz." It was clear that Rich had been in the thick of battle on the very front lines.

"Does Aunt Winifred know?" Scooter asked quietly.

The old man merely shook his head. She was working at a factory job assembling mufflers and wouldn't be home until later in the afternoon.

Directly under the headline was a picture of a serviceman. The copy under the picture read:

TONY LA PENNA MISSING IN ACTION

Sgt. Anthony La Penna, known to his many friends here as Tony, who was an aerial gunner, is missing in action over Germany according to a telegram which has been received from the government by his parents. The message stated the young man has been missing since Oct. 25. He had been overseas about a month...

Scooter went to the kitchen to get an apple to eat on the way back to school and picked up his gym bag.

"Good luck on your tryouts, sweetie," his mother said as he came through the kitchen on his way out the door.

"I might be late tonight."

"We'll keep your supper warm for you," she called after him. "Do good!"

Scooter tossed a "Thanks" over his shoulder. As he closed the storm door, Scooter was thinking about Tony—whatever his name was—missing in action. He supposed reading about one more in a long line of servicemen from little old Grand Harbor who had been killed or listed as missing in action would make him scared. It didn't. He was focused on getting into the service. He wanted to be part of the war, defeating Hitler if he was sent to the ETO or ToJo if he were sent to the Pacific. He couldn't wait to get his hands on a bomb-sight over some enemy bomb factory—which reminded him of Bergie's grandfather. He took a bite out his apple. Could he pull the trigger if he knew Bergie's grandfather was in that factory?

"Scooter! Wait up!"

Scooter turned to see Woodrow Nelson, forever known to his friends and family as Woody, loaded down with books and a gym bag as he ran to catch up.

Scooter waited for his friend. Woody was the class brain who would have gladly traded half his brilliant mind for half of Scooter's talents on the athletic field. The older Scooter got, the more he thought it might be a good trade.

"Why did you take all your textbooks home for lunch?" Scooter said as Woody approached.

"These aren't textbooks. They're for-pleasure books that are due at the library today or I'll get fined, and you know how obstreperous ol' man Klinger is about collecting overdue library fines."

"Ob- what?" Scooter asked as they resumed their walk to school.

"Obstreperous. You know, 'noisily and stubbornly defiant.'"

"Oh, that 'out-of-step-or-else.' I knew that. Here, let me help you with some of those books. Are these any I should be reading? *Paradise Lost* by John Milton. Is it any good? What's this . . . a German book?"

"It's a grammar book. I want to be able to speak it if I get shot down over Germany. Not that I intend on getting shot down, you understand. But I'm teaching it to myself. It's not so bad if you get the hang of it. But there sure are a lot of big words."

"It should be right up your alley, then. Is out-of-step-or-else one of those big German words?"

"Actually obstreperousness in German is *Widerspenstigkeit.* It has 17 letters, one more than obstreperousness. One of the few times the English word is almost as long as the German."

"I knew that, too."

They walked in silence for a while before Woody brought up the subject that was on both their minds—the basketball tryouts. "Do you think I have a chance of making the team?"

"If vocabulary tests were a part of the tryouts, you'd be starting center."

"Seriously, Scoot, I want it so bad I can't hardly sleep at night."

"Woody, if it were up to me, I'd have you on the team just because of what you know about the game. I think you'd make a great coach sometime."

"I don't want to be a coach sometime, Scoot. I want to make the basketball team now."

"I know, Woody, I know. So do I."

"Got any advice besides grow six inches during sixth hour?"

"My grandfather always says to play within yourself."

"What does that mean?" Woody wondered.

"Well, he thinks that doing the things you can do well is better than trying to do things you can't do."

Woody thought about that for a while and then sighed. "I'm doomed. My only chance of making the team is to show Coach Coors I can do the things I'm incapable of. Maybe I can talk Dutchie and some of the other guys from last year's team into leaving for the army this afternoon. Coors will have to take me then," he said as they entered the school doors just as the bell rang signaling the end of lunch hour.

*****

There were 16 hopeful young men in the boys' locker room after school. For Donald "Dutchie" Nagtzaam, Lester "Doolie" Higgins, Bergie, and Scooter this was just the start of another sports season. Football had ended a few weeks before and they had been starters. Basketball was the next step in the sports calendar that ended with baseball in the spring. These boys had previously been starting players for the Pirates, and a starting place now in their senior year was virtually assured. Others had been preparing for this since they were old enough to dribble a basketball. But while they were hopeful they would be among the four more players to be chosen to round out this year's varsity squad of eight players, they weren't sure. Their hopes had been heightened when Petey Schroder and Gary Slatski had left for the service the day after they turned 18, opening up two spots.

Several others of the boys putting on their gym clothes were there hoping beyond hope. Woody was among these. Not that he couldn't do the math. There were 16 players in the locker room and eight spots on the team, four of which were sure to be taken by Bergie, Dutchie, Doolie, and Scooter. That left 12 guys battling for the other four spots—not good odds, especially if you were only five-foot-six and considered a brain, not an athlete. How could he be cursed with such a blessing?

But Woody wanted to make the team. As a senior, this was his last chance, and it was not his nature to go down without a fight. He cinched the laces on his gym shoes down tight and was prepared to take them on, all 15 of them. Here I come, ready or not, he thought.

*****

"When do you suppose Coors is going to make the first cuts?" Woody wondered out loud as they left the school building after practice.

"If he does it like he's done it before, there will be 12 names on the bulletin board invited back for tryouts when we get to school in the morning," Dutchie said. "I'll see you guys. I gotta get to work."

"See ya, Dutchie, Scooter," were the replies. Dutchie and Scooter broke away from the group; Dutchie to pump gas and wash windshields at Pool's Service Station and Scooter to drive the delivery truck for Cashmere's Grocery and Meat Market.

It was Woody and Doolie that turned the other direction and began their trek home. They had become friends in the past few years. Doolie had once been the town bully, and Woody, who was always small for his age, was often on the receiving end. Although Woody hadn't forgotten, and Doolie still had a mean streak, both had matured and now managed to get along.

"How'd you think I played, Doolie?" Woody was looking for a sign that he might have played well enough to make the team.

"You did okay."

"No, Doolie, tell me honestly. No crap. How'd I do?"

"Woodrow," Doolie lapsed into an old habit of calling Woody by his full name when he was exasperated with him. "If it were up to me, I'd keep you on the team even if you weren't good enough to play a minute. You out-worked, out-hustled, and out-thought nearly every player on the floor today. But . . ."

"But what? But what, Doolie? Give it to me, I can take it. But what?"

They walked a few moments in silence.

"Woody, the plain truth is there are eight or nine guys bigger than you who can put the ball in the basket better than you."

"So you're saying I'm not good enough. You're saying that hard work and hustle and being smart don't matter for much."

"Hey, don't put words into my mouth. I think there are plenty of schools that would kill to have you. We just happen to have a powerhouse team this year."

They reached the street corner where a big bundle of newspapers lay. This was the beginning point of Doolie's paper route. Doolie stopped and turned to Woody.

"Half the guys in the gym today were starters last year, some of them as sophomores, too. You picked a bad time to be born and a horrible place to live if you wanted to play high school basketball."

Woody looked into Doolie's eyes and saw the truth of what he was saying. He turned away and began walking home to hide his disappointment.

"Hey! Don't be sore at me. You asked me and I told you. By the way," Doolie called after him, "did you figure out the answer to the take-home math problem?"

"In my head," Woody muttered under his breath without looking back. "In my head."

Chapter 3

The Tests

There were no acorns left on the sidewalk from the point where Woody left Doolie all the way to the Nelson house. For Woody, they had become Coach Coors and the players who, as Doolie had put it, were "bigger than you and who can put the ball in the basket better than you," and one by one Woody had kicked them mightily to the curb.

Woody had read somewhere that if you acted out your anger at someone by an activity on something else, you would feel better yourself and about the person you were angry with. The book had called it transference. But transferring the anger he felt about not being good enough to make the basketball team to the acorns on the sidewalk in his path didn't have the intended effect. When he got home, he was still seething.

"Good afternoon, Woody. How was school?" His mother was peeling potatoes for their dinner and the smell of roasting meat filled the kitchen.

When Woody didn't answer, she looked up and read the anger in his eyes. "Did you get cut already, honey?"

"Not yet."

"Well, if you're not cut yet, isn't there hope?"

"I'm not going to make it, Ma. I'm not good enough."

Sarah Nelson put down the potato she was peeling and came over to her son. "You can't be good at everything, honey. Nobody is. And I'll bet not one of those other boys has the good grades you do."

"Right now, I don't want to have the best grades in the school. I want to make the basketball team." He tried to make his voice sound defiant, fearing that the bitterness inside might come out in tears if he wasn't careful.

"Oh, honey," she said as she wrapped her arms around him. "Whatever happens, I want you to know I love you and I'm proud of you. And so's your father."

He allowed himself to remain encased in his mother's arms for several moments before he pulled away. "What's for supper? Where'd you get the meat? I thought we were out of rationing stamps for meat."

"We are, but Grandpa Nelson stopped by. He went hunting this morning and shot some rabbits. There'll be no dessert, though. We're out of sugar stamps and won't be able to get any until the end of the month. Canned peaches will have to do."

Because of the war effort, almost everything was in short supply. To prevent the shortages from causing prices to go so high that only the rich could buy necessary items, the government set up the Office of Price Administration, or the OPA. Everything from automobile tires and gas to sugar and meat fell under the control of the OPA.

The OPA issued rationing books to each household. A shopper needed to bring the coupon book to the store along with money to buy goods. Families had to be very selective about how much they used and how they planned their meals. Most families had garden plots called Victory Gardens in their yards. They were encouraged to grow more than they could eat and preserve the rest by canning.

Preserving things was a necessity. One of the tires on the Nelsons' 1939 Ford had so many patches on its inner tube that Woody's father often joked that none of the original tube was left, just patches. If a family ran out of something, they supplemented by other means, such as fishing or hunting as Grandfather Nelson had, or by fixing and patching, or by simply doing without.

"Any word from Uncle Lou?" Woody asked.

Mrs. Nelson shook her head, and at that moment there was a thud at the front door. "That'll be Doolie delivering the *Tribune*. Will you be a dear and get it and look for news about the Philippines?"

Woody temporarily forgot about basketball as he went to fetch the newspaper from the front porch and brought it into the living room. He kneeled down and spread the paper out on the floor and began a systematic review of the news of the war. The headlines told of General Patton's Third Army encircling the German fortress town of Metz. The story of the war in the Pacific came under a headline:

YANKS ON LEYTE BATTLE JAPS IN RAGING TYPHOON

Weary, water-soaked American infantrymen fought in a raging 100-mile-an-hour typhoon on the slippery ridges of northern Leyte Island today against fresh Japanese soldiers whose arrogant new commander boasted he would demand "unconditional surrender" of Gen. Douglas MacArthur. Infantrymen of the 24th Division, who have been fighting since they landed in the Philippines Oct. 20, made no gains but still held the offensive...

"Uncle Lou" was Pfc. Louis Andrews, Woody's mother's brother. Sarah Nelson was very close to her brother. She called him Sluggo, he called her Sweetcakes. Lou had enlisted in the service long before the war broke out and had been one of 15,000 men stationed at the American army base on Corregidor in the Bataan peninsula of the Philippines. On May 6, 1942,

11,500 men in the Corregidor base surrendered to an invading Japanese army after a fierce battle. That's all the American public knew.

The 11,500 men who survived the fighting were marched 55 miles to a train that would take them to a prisoner of war camp. During this march, 2,330 men died. None of the families of those soldiers knew if their loved ones were killed in the defense of Corregidor, died in what came to be called the Bataan Death March, or survived and were now in the prisoner of war camp. Their hope was that the Americans could recapture the Philippine Islands and liberate the POW camps. So they listened to the radio, read the newspapers, and waited for some breakthrough.

Another headline caught Woody's eye:

SGT. A. BROWNE MISSING IN ACTION

Sgt. Arnold "Brownie" Browne, U.S. Army, is missing in action in France according to a telegram which has been received by his mother, Mrs. Emma Browne of Robbins Road. The message stated the young soldier was reported missing on Oct. 24...

Woody knew Brownie. He was a senior when Woody was a sophomore. Brownie was a big strapping kid, the kind who could do anything and seemed invincible. Now he was most likely a casualty of the war. Woody finished reading the paper and reported to his mom that there was very little news about the fighting in the Philippines. Their waiting would continue.

*****

At the Secory house that evening, Scooter ate his supper, while the older family members sipped their coffee. He listened to them hash and rehash the latest war news before dropping a bomb of his own.

"Dutchie and I have decided to take the Air Corps tests to see if we can get into aviator school."

Aunt Winifred gasped. Scooter's mother just put her hand to her mouth and looked at her son in disbelief.

"You mean Air Corpse," Russell interjected.

"The *corps* in Air Corps is pronounced like the *core* of an apple," their father corrected. "It's the Army Air Core."

A heavy, awkward silence followed, and Scooter knew it was a mistake to blurt out his news as he did. But it was done and the announcement was made. Grandfather Secory saved him.

"You figure if you pass the tests, you can pick your services instead of being drafted and taking your chances?"

Scooter turned to his grandfather. "Dutchie's looked into it some. He's been to the Air Corps recruiter in

Muskegon and they told him there's a good chance we can get into flight school."

"Oh, Peter!" Scooter's mother addressed his father. "He's just a boy. Surely..." she stopped at the words. She knew full well that the young men who were leaving on the train or the bus nearly every week for some part of the service or another were all little more than boys. It's just that Scooter was her boy.

"I think Scooter is making sense, Ruthie. It's five, six months until he graduates and then he'll be off to the war whether he does his choosing or they choose for him. Much as I don't want him to go, he needs to do his duty same as everyone else."

Scooter was pleased to get his father's support. He had counted on it. He turned to Grandfather Secory, who winked at him before he spoke.

"I think you'll make a fine aviator, Scoot. And when you get out, I think there'll be plenty of jobs in commercial aviation. Unless I miss my guess, planes will take over from trains for a lot of the traveling passengers, and there will be a big need for pilots. When are you going to take these tests?"

"The Air Corps recruiter is coming to school tomorrow. We're going to take them during fourth hour."

When she heard those words, Ruth Secory collected her coffee cup and saucer and got up from the table.

Without saying a word, she left the kitchen and climbed the stairs to her bedroom. Scooter pushed his chair back and went to follow her, but Grandfather Secory held his arm out to stop him.

"Let her go. We all have to handle the war in our own way. You feel the need to go off to war and do something. Just like your Uncle Rich . . ."

At that point, Aunt Winifred quickly picked up her dishes and also retreated up the stairs. They heard her knock on the door of Scooter's parents' bedroom. When they heard the door close behind her, Grandfather Secory continued.

"The women folk need to handle it their way. I'm not sure yet who has it the worst, those that get to see the war or those who wait to see the war heroes. But it ain't anyone's idea of a picnic any which way. Your mother understands you need to go. She knew this announcement of yours was coming sooner or later. She . . . we all would rather it came later. I hope you can understand that."

Scooter turned back toward the table and sat down. They were all quiet for a few moments. Then Scooter's father thought to ask, "How did basketball tryouts go?"

*****

"Did you tell your parents we're going to take the Air Corps tests today?" Dutchie asked Scooter as they made their way to school the next morning.

"Yep."

"How'd they take it?"

"They understand, but my mom doesn't want to think about it. D'you tell your folks?" asked Scooter.

"No. They have enough on their minds worrying about Rich. They don't need to think about me going until they have to. One star in the window is enough. Winn get any more letters?"

"The one a couple of days ago. Nothing yesterday. You get any?"

"Nope," replied Dutchie. "The paper last night said that the Third Army was at Metz. That got my ma upset and all. I don't know what's worse—not knowing where he is, or knowing where he is and that it's in the middle of the shooting."

"Speaking of shooting, you going to the Rifle Club meeting tomorrow?" asked Scooter.

"What are they meeting about?" Dutchie wanted to know.

"There's so many guys joining, they need to get some more rifles. They're gonna ask the Rotary Club for a donation to get ten more rifles," Scooter said as they reached the front door of the high school.

As they opened the door, a slender girl with honey brown hair and dark brown flashing eyes came bouncing down the stairs to meet them. "Congratulations, you two. You're both on the list!" she said excitedly.

"List . . .?" was all that Scooter could get out of his mouth before Casey rushed on.

"The basketball tryout list, silly, as if you weren't thinking about it." She slid between the two boys and hooked her arms into the crooks of theirs, almost propelling them down the hall toward the bulletin board.

"Actually, we hadn't thought about it," Scooter said honestly as they approached the board. The cluster of students around it stepped aside as the trio approached, realizing that the list was more important to the two boys than it was to them. The notice read:

THE FOLLOWING STUDENTS ARE INVITED TO THE BASKETBALL TRYOUTS AT 3:15 THIS AFTERNOON IN THE GYM:

Berilla, David
Denton, Carl
Greenberg, Samuel
Higgins, Lester
Merrill, Jacob
Nagtzaam, Donald
Peters, Marvin
Secory, Gregory
Van Doorn, Percival
Westerhoff, Eugene
Witham, Robert
Woodrow, Nelson

- Coach Coors

Scooter read off the names, "Chappie, Bub, Bergie, Doolie, Jake, Dutchie, Marv, me, Red, Westie, Packy, and Woody! Well, well. The little bugger made it this far. I hope Coach Coors keeps him."

There were two other announcements pinned to the bulletin board. One said the Army Air Corps aviation test would be administered in the home economics room during fourth hour. The other said that the Rifle Club would be meeting tomorrow. Members were reminded that if their rifles were not already at school, they needed to bring them tomorrow for the club picture for the school year book.

The trio turned toward their lockers. "You still planning to take the aviation test, Scoot?" Casey wanted to know as they walked along.

"I'm signed up for it. So's Dutchie . . ."

At that moment, they nearly bumped into Woody, coming around a corner. A scowl had replaced his usual impish grin.

"Oops, sorry," Woody said. "I wasn't watching where I was going." He tried to walk around Scooter, but Scooter sidestepped into his path.

"Why the sour puss?"

Woody didn't even look up. "Some days you're the dog; some days you're the hydrant. Today I feel like the hydrant after the dog stopped by."

“What happened? You hear about your Uncle Lou?”

“No, I heard about the basketball team.”

“What about it? Aren’t you happy about it?” asked Scooter.

“What’s to be happy about? I got cut.”

Scooter and Dutchie looked at each other in amazement. It was Casey who said, “Cut? But your name’s on the list. You didn’t get cut.”

Woody looked up. “You funnin’ me? I saw the list, my name’s not on it.”

“Is too,” and “Tis so,” Scooter and Dutchie said at the same time.

“If you’re funnin’ me, so help me . . .,” Woody stopped in mid-sentence. He could see his friends were serious. He burst through them and made for the bulletin board. At first he saw what he had seen before. The list was alphabetical and if he were on it, Nelson should have come after Nagtzaam and before Peters. And it wasn’t there. He was about to accuse his friends of a cruel joke when he saw it. His name was last, put up as “Woodrow, Nelson” instead of “Nelson, Woodrow.” He wasn’t cut after all!

“SHE-AH-ZAM!” he blurted out just as the bell rang calling the students to their first hour classes.

*****

The Army Air Corps recruiting officer stood ramrod

straight and tall at the front of the home economics room. There were ten young hopefuls sitting at tables around the room. Scooter and Dutchie were there as well as Lou Breitels, Gump Casemier, Rog Dahlman, Dell DeGram, Ole Olson, Hex Hecksel, Nemo Niemazak, and Woody. The recruiter began.

"Gentlemen. On behalf of the United States Army Air Corps, I want to thank you for volunteering to be tested for possible enlistment in the Corps. You should know at the outset that the standards for the Air Corps are very high. Many young men volunteer to be tested, but only a few are chosen. This is because the requirements for pilots, bombardiers, gunners, aircraft care and maintenance are very high, and the Corps must be very selective.

"The Corps is looking for specific mental, emotional, and physical characteristics. You may well be smart enough, but not have the right emotional or physical make up, and two out of the three are not enough. If you do not meet these requirements, it doesn't mean you are not fit to serve your country in another important capacity. But as I said, the Corps is very selective.

"The test is 90 minutes long. It is designed to test your ability to think clearly and react quickly. It is also designed to find out something about your emotional make-up. For some questions, there are no right or wrong answers. An example of this type of question is: If you come to a puddle in the sidewalk, do you A) jump over it, B) walk around it, C) walk through it, or D) go back home to get your rubbers."

There was nervous laughter from the students.

"I'm going to pass these out. Do not open the booklet until I tell you. When you are finished, bring your completed test up to me and you are dismissed. Please raise your hand when I call your name. Louis Frederick Breitels. Robert John Casemier . . ."

Woody looked at the clock on the wall after he had answered the last question and closed the test booklet. It was only 50 minutes since the test started. Everyone else was busy writing or figuring. He looked across the isle where Gump Casemier sat and determined that Gump was only about halfway through the test. He debated whether he should go back and re-check his answers. But what was right: A) jump over the puddle or B) walk around it? He decided he had done as well as he could and left the table, handing the test booklet to the sergeant. The recruiter looked at his watch and wrote the time on the booklet cover. He then rose from his seat and walked to the door. Woody thought he motioned for him to follow.

When they were in the hall, the recruiter seemed to be walking away from Woody when suddenly he turned and threw up his hand as if he were going to strike Woody! Startled, Woody instinctively threw up his hands and went into a fighter's crouch. When he realized that the sergeant wasn't attacking him but had just turned suddenly and was scratching his chin, Woody felt foolish and dropped his guard.

"Sorry, sir. For a minute I thought you were going to . . . ah . . . well . . ."

"No need to be sorry, Mr. Nelson. No need at all. Thanks for testing for the Air Corps." With no explanation, he left Woody standing in the hall and went back into the classroom.

Although he rarely felt stupid, Woody was sure he had just made the biggest blunder of his young life. His chances of becoming a fighter pilot had just disappeared into the home economics room! Woodrow Nelson had almost attacked an Army Air Corps recruiting sergeant for scratching his chin!

Woody didn't wait for the noon dismissal bell. He got his coat and began walking home, kicking acorns all the way.

When the recruiting sergeant got back to his office later that day, he was greeted by his secretary.

"Well, sergeant, did you find anyone in Grand Harbor High School who might help you to fill any of your quotas?"

"I just might have," he responded with a satisfied chuckle. "I just might have found a fighter pilot. Gutsy little kid. Fits the size requirement. He finished the test in 50 minutes. That's a record as far as I know. Score the top test first and let me know the results."

Chapter 4

Slam Dunks Not Allowed!

November 12, 1944
Somewhere in the ETO

To my darling wife:

I'm writing from well behind the front. We were moved back for a bath and some clean clothes. My company hasn't had a chance for a bath or clean clothes for 32 days and that's a long time in the same underwear and socks. With the mud we've been in, I'm afraid I'll never get really clean again. I've developed a mild case of trench foot. Fortunately, or unfortunately, it's not bad enough to keep me out of the war. Some of the fellas have it so bad they're being taken to the hospital, which I'm told is some 49 miles farther back. One of my buddies from my original company just rejoined us. He spent 60 days in a French hospital recovering from a bullet in the hip. So we lose some and we gain some.

If ever you needed a sign that I will make it through this war, it came the day before yesterday. We were walking down a trench looking for a break in our telephone wires when I stepped on a mine. I felt the plunger go all the way down to the pin and my heart sank right with it. I thought I had bought the farm, but thank God it was a dud. I actually looked down to see if I really had my leg. We all walked on the side of the trench after that.

I miss you so very much. Say hello to everyone. I pray daily that you are doing okay. I know you're in good hands at 49465 Howard Street. God bless you and keep me until we meet again. I love you so very much and I miss you just as much.

Rich

"Have you figured out where Uncle Rich is, Gramps?" Scooter asked between bites of his grilled cheese sandwich that noon.

"Metz. According to the papers, the Third Army had flushed out the last resistance in Metz by the middle of November, so that might explain why there was a break and he was able to get some relief," his grandfather answered.

"I can't imagine going 32 days without a bath or a change of clothes—even your underwear—and in those conditions. I shudder to think what that must be like," Scooter's mother said, closing her eyes and actually shuddering at the thought.

"We pray for Uncle Rich every day. Too bad we can't take a bath for him," Russell said. Then he looked at his mother and added, "Not that I want to take any more baths, y'unnerstand."

"Whew," Grandfather Secory pretended to wipe his brow. "I'm glad you added that last part. Offering to take a bath for someone else! For a minute there I was wondering who you were and what you were doing in Russell Secory's body."

"Does Aunt Winnie know we got a letter?"

"I phoned Oldbergs and left a message. Then she called back on her break and asked me to open it and read it to her. I'm worried for her. I don't think she gets a wink of sleep for worrying whether he's dead or alive. She says she doesn't know what she'd do if her mind wasn't occupied with her work during the day."

"He'll be okay," Grandfather Secory said quietly. "Rich'll be okay."

At those words, Ruth Secory's eyes began to fill with tears, and she got up from the table and ran upstairs to the bedroom and closed the door behind her. There was only the tinkle of silverware against dishes and the sounds of eating for a few moments.

Grandfather Secory cleared his throat. "How did the Air Corps test go, Scooter?"

"Okay, I guess. A lot of it is trick questions. You don't know what answer they're looking for so it's hard to know how you did."

"What do you mean, trick questions, Scoot?" Russell wanted to know.

"Oh, like, there was one that said a small child is alone in a car and releases the parking brake, and the car begins to roll on a path that will take it out onto a busy street. Do you: get out of the way, try to stop the oncoming traffic, try to get in the car and stop it, or go call your father for help?"

Russell thought for a moment. "Jeesh. What is the right answer?"

"Never leave a small child alone in a car," the old man answered. Russell sputtered and sent bits of grilled cheese sandwich spraying over the table. Their laughter was interrupted by a sharp knock on the back door. Before they could wonder who it was or move to answer the door, they got their answer.

"Yoo-hoo, anybody home?"

It was the Widow Bach, for whom everyone else's back door carried a big sign visible only to her that read "JUST WALK RIGHT IN, YOOHOOING APPRECIATED BUT NOT NECESSARY." She had become heavy in her later years and she was wheezing. Scooter offered her his chair, and she sat down heavily.

"Baked a batch of my double fudge brownies. Know how you like 'em sa'much. I see you're finished with your lunch so these won't spoil your appetite. He'p yerself. Hear about the Boven woman over in Spring

Lake? She's tellin' folks she's seen her son get wounded somewheres in Europe in her dreams. Hasn't heard from him in a while. 'Course God knows what mighta happened to him and all, but saying she was there . . . ." At that point she drew circles around her ear with her index finger as if to say "loony."

Merrill Secory got up and picked up his dishes. "I know Johanna Boven," he said. "As I recall, she can recite much of the Book of Psalms by heart and a lot of other poetry and long passages of Shakespeare. If her mind is crazy, we could all use a little crazy. I need to go out to pick up some things from the store, so if you guys are finished, I'll drive you back to school," he continued as he put his dishes in the sink. The two boys took his cue and followed.

The Widow Bach was cackling on as they fled out the door.

*****

The boy's locker room wasn't as tense as it had been the first night of basketball tryouts. There was some laughter and good-natured teasing. But Woody hadn't quite gotten over the experience with the recruiting officer and wasn't in the best of humor. Scooter noticed Woody was off in a corner, not joining in the banter.

"Woody, you got one of your profound Questions of the Day for us to contemplate before we take to the court?" Scooter asked.

Woody didn't look up but continued to tie his gym shoes.

"Come on, Woody, wha'cha got for us?" and "We could use some intellectual material before practice," the boys prodded him.

"You know, guys, I been thinking," Chappie Berilla said. "Mebbe we should call him Nelly instead of Woody."

"Nelly? Why Nelly?" Westie wanted to know.

"Because Coach Coors obviously thinks his name is Nelson. You know, on the list on the bulletin board. Woodrow comma Nelson instead of Nelson comma Woodrow. So instead of Woody, it should be Nelly."

"Good one, Chappie. Nelly. I like the sound of it," Doolie joined in. "But it would never do. Everyone would confuse him with Jennella Kistler. Isn't her nickname Nelly?"

"They are about the same height, but there shouldn't be any confusion. Jennella's hair is longer and she wears lipstick on Saturday nights," Marv chimed in.

At that Woody stood up and took a swipe at Marv.

"Okay," he said. "You wisenheimers are such know-it-alls, tell me this. Is there another word that sounds like *homonym* but has a different meaning?"

The locker room was silent for a moment as the players thought about Woody's Question of the Day. Then

Jake Merrill began to snicker, then Scooter, then Dutchie as they got the joke in Woody's question.

"I don't get it. What's so funny?" Chappie wanted to know.

"You're not the sharpest stick in the bundle, are you Berilla," Scooter said with a wink at Woody as he got up to lead the team to the gym. "You should learn not to play with dogs you can't run with. Come on guys. Let's go do it!"

*****

Before Coach Coors came in to begin the practice, the players practiced their two-handed set shots and their underhanded free throws in a semi-circle around the basket. Bergie and Woody were under the basket getting rebounds.

"Bergie, if I were as tall as you, I'd take the ball and just go up and slam it straight down through the hoop. Why take a chance on a bad carom off the backboard? Just slam it through," said Woody.

"What to do you mean, slam it through?"

"You know, like you were dunking someone's head under water. Dunk the ball down through the hoop."

"I don't think I can jump high enough to do that. But . . ." At that point a rebound came to him and he held up his hand for the shooters to stop for a moment. He eyed the rim and took a couple of steps back of the basket. He took two steps, recoiled his body, and jumped as high as he could. With the ball in two hands, he tried to get it over the rim and slam it down through the hoop. The ball made it over the front of the rim but rattled the far side of the hoop and bounced out.

"What'cha trying to do, Bergie?" Doolie asked.

"Woody has the idea to just slam dunk the ball through the hoop without using the backboard." By that time he had another ball, took a couple of steps back and tried it again. Again he got the ball over the rim, but it hit the backside of the rim. It rattled around but popped out again.

"You have to be able to have your hand on top of the ball when you try to dunk it down," Woody instructed.

Dutchie had a ball and walked up. He eyed the rim, took a running start and leaped as high as he could with the ball in one hand. As the ball cleared the rim, Dutchie slammed it downward through the hoop. There was a chorus of "hurrahs" and "atta boys" from the other players.

Not to be outdone, Bergie got a running start and managed to slam the ball through the hoop, but not with as much finesse as Dutchie. Doolie grabbed a ball and approached the basket. But even with a running start, he couldn't get up high enough and the ball got trapped between the outer part of the rim and his hand. Bergie tried it again. This time he did it with a little more grace. Westie stepped up with a ball to try it when a voice boomed and reverberated through the gym.

"IF I EVER CATCH ANY OF YOU TRYING A STUPID STUNT LIKE THAT AGAIN, THAT PERSON WILL NEVER PLAY BASKETBALL FOR ME. HAVE I MADE MYSELF CLEAR?"

Nobody moved and except for a loose basketball that was bouncing out its kinetic energy, there wasn't a sound. The gym had an old wooden floor, and as Coach Coors walked toward them, the creaking floor was the only sound to be heard.

Woody noticed nobody was breathing and nobody looked up. The sounds of "We are the Pirates, the mighty, mighty Pirates . . ." from the cheerleaders' practice came echoing down the halls and through the cracks in the gym doors. Woody wondered if Coach Coors had been watching long enough to know that he had started the slam-dunking. That could end his chances to make the team, even if he were much taller.

Coach Coors made his way to the front of the semicircle. He stood there for a moment looking at his players, one by one. Woody thought he looked especially long and hard at him. Then the coach spoke, very deliberately.

"Basketball is a game of teamwork and a game of

skill. It's a gentleman's game. It is not a circus act. Stunts like I've just witnessed have no place in the game. I trust I've made myself clear?"

Woody thought some of the guys still hadn't breathed.

"Good, then let's get started, gentlemen."

*****

"Hi, Mom. Did we hear from Uncle Lou?" The question was the same every night.

"Oh, Woody, it's you. No, honey, no word. Listen, I'm late with supper tonight. I was down to the armory rolling bandages and we got carried away with the time. Would you be a real honey and set the table for me. We're having rabbit stew with the leftovers from last night. How did your day go, honey?"

"Fine, Mom. Just fine." In fact, if you didn't count the time he almost attacked the Air Corps recruiting officer for scratching his chin and the incident over the slam-dunking, his day was almost perfect. About the only thing that went right was that he was the only person in solid geometry class to get the take-home problem right—and he had done it in his head at that. But solving solid geometry problems in your head didn't matter a fiddle or a fig if what you really wanted was to be a fighter pilot and make the basketball team.

He finished setting the table in time to hear the thud

of the evening paper hitting the front porch. He went to check on the news of the war in the Pacific.

The headlines read:

SUPER-FORTRESSES HIT TOKYO IN FORCE

B-29s Strike from Saipan;

Japs Report 70 Planes

General Arnold Says: "Attack Will Be Carried on Relentlessly from the Air Until the Day of the Land-Sea Invasion of Japan's Home Islands": Is First Bombing Since Doolittle's Raid

There was a smaller headline in another column:

32nd Seizes Limon, Pursues Jap Forces Beyond City

Mud-Splattered Division Lunges Southward After Capturing Bastion in Climax to Leyte Campaign

The Japanese 1st Division has been practically destroyed, Gen. MacArthur said in announcing that the Yankee 32nd had smashed into Limon yesterday after a typhoon-slowed battle.

Between the two columns was a picture of a soldier under the caption:

KILLED IN ITALY

Pfc. Russell Walker, son of Mr. and Mrs. Leonard C. Hudson of Ferrysburg, was killed in action Nov. 2 in Italy, according to word received by his wife, Jesse.

"We're bombing Tokyo, Mom," Woody said as he came back into the kitchen. "And it appears we're starting to make progress in the Philippines. And Russ Walker has been killed in Italy."

"Isn't that the young man who used to pump gas at Swede's gas station in Ferrysburg?"

Woody nodded. "I think so."

Mrs. Nelson took a deep breath and wiped her hands on her apron.

"We're getting too many Gold Star Mothers. There were three of them rolling bandages at the armory this afternoon. My heart goes out to them so. I couldn't bear the thought of losing my son."

Woody decided it was not the time to tell her that he had taken the Air Corps test that morning and that he dreamed of becoming a fighter pilot, a dream that most likely was dashed when he almost attacked the recruiting officer. Now he may never have to tell her.

Woody had hoped the day would come when his family would hang a small white flag in their front window with one blue star for their son who was serving his country. And he wanted his parents to say that their son, Woodrow, was a fighter pilot in the Army Air Corps. But he also knew his dream could well become his mother's nightmare—becoming a Gold Star Mother whose son lost his life in serving his country.

Just then, Meyer Nelson came home for dinner. Woody went into the kitchen to greet his father.

*****

The conversation at the Secory's dinner table was much lighter. They had received the letter from Rich that morning, and even though the letter had been written two weeks before, its arrival made it seem as if he were alive and well.

Scooter was relating the story of the slam dunk incident at practice.

"Just then Coach Coors said at the top of his voice, 'If I ever catch any of you trying a stupid trick like that again, you'll never play basketball for me.'"

"As you describe it, it seems like a sensible thing to do if a fella could jump that high," Grandfather Secory observed. "Who came up with that idea?"

"Woody."

"Woodrow Nelson?" Scooter's mother asked. "He's such a nice boy. I'm glad to hear he's made the basketball team. He tries so hard and he always seems to be on the fringes of your sports. I remember back in Boy Scout baseball, he had to hide in right field. Didn't I read in the paper he went on to become an Eagle Scout?"

"We hid him in right field, Ma. And he hasn't made the team yet, this is just the second day of tryouts. I hope he makes it. He knows a lot about the game and he's darn smart. He can also be very funny. He has these Questions of the Day that he pops on you that make you laugh and think at the same time."

"Like what questions?" Russell wanted to know.

"Oh, like one I remember was 'Can a cross-eyed teacher ever control her pupils?'"

There were chortles around the table.

"Today," Scooter continued, "the Question of the Day was 'Is there a word that sounds like *homonym* that has a different meaning?'"

Aunt Winifred was the first to laugh at that, and the others sitting at the table realized it was the first time they had heard her laugh in a very long time.

"What's a harmonium?" Russell didn't get the joke.

"HOM-o-nym means a word that sounds the same as another word but has a different meaning, like *knight* and *night*, and *to* and *two*, too." Winnie laughed at her own play on words.

"You tell Woody," Grandfather said, peering over his reading glasses at Scooter, "that you'll give him another word that sounds like *homonym* but has a different meaning after he gives you another word for *synonym*."

"Good one, Gramps. He'll like that one," Scooter said with a laugh and a nod of his head in appreciation.

"All this is too much humming and sinning for me," Russell declared. And at that, they all had a good laugh.

Scooter decided this was no time to bring up the Air Corps test he had taken that morning. Light-hearted moments like this didn't come very often, and they were far too precious to interrupt.

*****

There were no such smiles at the Greenbergs' dinner table that evening. The last letter they received was dated over four months ago. With each passing day, the chances they would hear from or about their dear relatives in Europe would lessen. The horrible possibility that Bergie's grandfather was making timing devices for Nazi bombs was never mentioned again. But it was not forgotten.

Chapter 5

Tryouts

There were two announcements on the bulletin board the next morning. The one that attracted the girls read:

A BIG SHINDIG IN THE GYM
SATURDAY NIGHT

THE SATURDAY NIGHT CLUB INVITES ALL STUDENTS TO ANOTHER FUN NIGHT OF DANCING, GAMES, & REFRESHMENTS IN THE GYM FROM 7:00 TO 9:30.

A jitterbug contest at 9:00 with gift certificates for free sodas at Presley's to the winners!

Live orchestra plus we have the new Glen Miller record!

Chaperones are Mr. Thoma,
Mr. & Mrs. Johnson and Mr. & Mrs. Mead

DON'T YOU DARE MISS IT!

The boys were more interested in another announcement:

> THE FOLLOWING STUDENTS ARE INVITED TO RETURN TO THE BASKETBALL TRYOUTS AT 3:15 THIS AFTERNOON IN THE GYM:
>
> Berilla, David
> Greenberg, Samuel
> Higgins, Lester
> Merrill, Jacob
> Nagtzaam, Donald
> Peters, Marvin
> Secory, Gregory
> Westerhoff, Eugene
> Woodrow, Nelson
>
> —Coach Coors

"Well, Woody, you're still hanging in there, buddy." Scooter slapped him on the back.

"Why do you think he puts me last and has my name backwards?" Woody asked.

"Oh, it's not enough that your name is on the list, now you want it spelled right?" Doolie teased. "I'd have thought it'd be enough to be listed as the-short-kid-who-tried-to-get-us-all-in-trouble-with-the-slam...ooof!"

Woody had elbowed Doolie in the solar plexus without turning around.

"Oh, Lester, were you standing there? I didn't see you as I was turning around. Did I hurt you? I'm so sorry!" Woody said this with a mocking tone of concern.

"You little rat, I ought to punch you in your snot locker right here and now," Doolie said menacingly.

"Doolie, you just got lucky. Ol' man Babcock is coming down the hall even as I speak. You know how the principal hates violence, so you just got spared the embarrassment of having me whup your sorry butt in front of all your friends." Then turning to the passing principal he said, "Good morning, Mr. Babcock."

"Good morning, Woodrow," and he nodded toward the rest of them, "...boys."

"Good morning, sir," they all replied, almost in unison just as the bell began ringing for the opening of classes.

"You gotta hand it to the little guy," Dutchie observed as he and Scooter headed for class. "Woody's not afraid to dish it out, even in the face of danger. Doolie's bigger'n him by must be 30 pounds and six inches. There was a time when Doolie would have cleaned his clock right then and there."

"He's gutsy, alright," Scooter responded. "But what makes him always see the glass as half empty?"

"What do you mean, see the glass half empty?"

"If there is a half a glass of milk and a person with

a positive outlook on life looks at it, he sees it as half full. A person who always sees the negative side of life sees the same glass as half empty. Woody always sees the glass as half empty, you know, like just now. He asked, 'Why is my name last' instead of saying 'Isn't it great that my name's on the list.'"

"I don't know. That's just Woody, I guess."

"My grandfather reads the letters from your brother Rich and is convinced he'll be all right. Winnie reads the same letter and thinks he's not gonna make it. I'm going off to win the war; my mother thinks I'll get shot down on my first mission."

"I know. My ma's the same way. It's as if any day now she'll have to go to the next Gold Star Mother's Club meeting," Dutchie said as they turned into their first hour classroom.

*****

There were no attempts to slam dunk the basketball during warm-ups that afternoon. Coach Coors had led Grand Harbor High to several state championships and was respected by everyone. Since they had been reprimanded, the players did not wish to irritate him again and listened more intently than usual.

"The farther away you are from the basket, the more chance you're going to miss the shot. The closer you are when you shoot, the more likely the shot will go in the basket. So, we're going to concentrate on working the ball in as close as we can for the high percentage shot. A lot of the drills we're going to be doing will be learning and executing set plays that, if done correctly and with precision, will get us the high percentage lay-up or dog shot we're looking for. Even though I haven't decided on the final cuts yet, we're going to begin regular practice tonight. Our first game of the season is not far away.

"Now, at the end of the season last year, I had a talk with each of you from last year's team and told you what I expected of you this season. Mr. Greenberg, what did I tell you I needed from you this season?"

Bergie shifted his feet and hesitated, then spoke. "A better hook shot, and I needed to be stronger in the pivot."

"That's right. I want you to demonstrate what a good, fundamental hook shot looks like."

"You mean right now?"

"Would you like us to wait around for this?" the coach asked raising his eyebrows.

"No, sir," was the quick reply. Bergie took a position about ten feet in front of the basket, facing the coach. With the ball in his right hand extended in front of him, Bergie started forward with his left foot, turned slightly to his left, and pushing off with his right foot, sent the ball up over his head in a graceful motion and banked the shot into the net.

"Good, Greenberg, very good. A good hook shot is a joy to behold. Notice the man who might be guarding him from behind has no chance to block the shot."

No, but a quick guard playing in front of him could knock the ball out of his hands the way he extends it out there unprotected like that, Woody thought to himself.

The coach had continued talking. "Now a left-handed hook shot, Greenberg."

Bergie took another pass and this time with the ball in his left hand, executed the play from the other direction. This time, however, the ball hit the rim and bounced out.

"Well, Greenberg's fundamentals are perfect. He has good form going in either direction. He just needs to practice his accuracy. Mr. Nagtzaam, what were you going to work on since the end of last season?"

Dutchie didn't hesitate, "I had to work on my set shot and my foot work. You said that I played basketball like a fullback. You wanted me to play tennis in the spring and work on becoming more nimble."

The thought of big Dutchie becoming nimble sent snickers through the rest of the players. Doolie found the idea particularly amusing but choked it off when

Coach Coors turned and gave him an evil-eye stare.

"That's right, Mr. Nagtzaam," the coach continued. "So take a ball and show us the proper form for the two-handed set shot."

Dutchie dribbled toward a spot just outside the free throw line, took the ball in both hands and arced a shot that dropped through the hoop with a swish.

"In my never-to-be-humble opinion, *swish* is the sweetest sound in sports," the coach said appreciatively. "I know some people like to hear the crack of a bat against a baseball, and some barbarians like to hear the clash of shoulder pads. But to me, the sound of *swish* is sweet. Let me hear it again, Mr. Nagtzaam, if you please."

Dutchie caught a ball from Scooter, dribbled a few steps to his right, stopped, and with two hands, arced another shot. This one hit the rim with a clang and bounced out.

"And that, gentlemen, is the harshest, most disappointing sound I know. *Clang* is the sound of a missed opportunity, a failed attempt. If you don't know it already, the sound of *swish* is so powerful it will make crowds rise to their feet in admiration and joy. The sound of *clang* will bring cries of disappointment and anguish. I intend to make *swish* the operative sound from this team. Let the rest of the league be clangers. I will make you men swishers."

Woody smiled at that. "I will make you men swishers" reminded him of a children's Sunday School song, "I Will Make You Fishers of Men." No one else smiled, missing the coach's play on words.

"Mr. Higgins," Coach Coors addressed Doolie next. "What were you to be working on in the off-season?"

"The left-handed lay-up?"

"If you're asking me a question, the answer is yes. You were to practice shooting the lay-up as well from the left side of the basket with your left hand as you do from the right side of the basket with your right hand. Would you demonstrate the proper technique for shooting lay-ups, or dog shots, for us?"

Doolie took off dribbling up to the right side of the basket and smoothly laid the ball up off the backboard and in. His attempt from the left was also successful, but it lacked the polish of his right-handed lay-up.

"Well, it appears that Mr. Higgins still has a way to go before he is as accomplished from the left side as he is from the right. Now, gentlemen, these are the shots we will be practicing, drilling into your minds and bodies until they become second nature to you."

For the next hour and 15 minutes, the boys did just that. If their technique was even slightly deficient, the coach blew his whistle and the offender was shown the error of his ways.

At quarter to five, Coach Coors blew his whistle loud and long. “Okay, gentlemen, let’s hit the showers. That’s it for today. Ah, Mr. Woodrow, I’d like to see you in my office for a moment.”

Hell’s bells, thought Woody, this is it. He’s gonna cut me. Woody didn’t turn around to see if his teammates were looking at him with sympathy or amusement.

The coach’s office was hardly bigger than a closet with a small desk and chair for the coach and a folding chair wedged between the edge of the desk and the wall. The coach motioned for Woody to sit down as he closed the door behind him.

“Mr. Woodrow, if I’m not mistaken, aren’t you the student who has been sitting in the balcony for the past two years or so for every basketball game and more than a few practices?”

“Yes.” Woody decided this was not the time to tell the coach his name was not Mr. Woodrow.

“I thought so.” The coached hesitated for a moment. Woody was certain he didn’t want to hear what the coach had to say.

“It was your idea to try stuffing the basketball straight down into the hoop the other day, wasn’t it?’

Hell’s double bells. The coach had seen it. Now his

goose was cooked. He couldn't think of anything or anyone to blame. "Yes, sir," Woody admitted meekly.

"Where did you get that idea?"

Woody didn't look up, he just gave the coach his "I-don't-know" shrug. Why didn't Coors just cut him and get it over with?

"Our first game is in a week and it's against Zeeland. I'm told they have a lot of tall fellas—big strong farm boys that can shoot the strings off the basket. How would you defend against them, Mr. Woodrow?"

What was this, a test? Woody wondered. He thought for a moment, but not about how he would answer. He knew exactly how he would defend against Zeeland. Instead he was thinking about whether he should answer at all. Finally, he decided he had nothing to lose. No doubt Coors had decided to cut him, and he might as well be broke as badly bent.

"I'd play my fastest and hardest working guards and put a full-court press on them. Typically big guys don't move the ball well, and I don't think they could handle a good full-court press. I'd substitute often and run those big farmers ragged."

"What if my fastest and hardest working guards were not my starters?"

"I'd play the best men for the job, not necessarily the best overall players."

The coach thought for a moment and smiled. It occurred to Woody the coach was having too much fun at his expense. But there was no place to hide in this tiny room, so he'd have to sweat out the game Coors was playing with him.

"The game after that is Grand Rapids Christian. They are a short team, very fast and scrappy. How would you defend against them?"

Again Woody hesitated. "I'd play my best shooters and shoot a lot more from the outside. Last year their speed didn't allow us to get the ball inside and we were flummoxed. I'd take the uncontested shots they give us from the outside and use our height and strength to get the rebounds for easy lay-ups if we miss.

"With all due respect, sir, your philosophy is to work the ball in for the high percentage shots. We get about 20 of those in a game and make 75 percent of them. That gives us 30 points. Why not shoot the ball 40 times and make half of them. That's 40 points. Then we can use our height to pick up the easy rebounds.

"Also, they'll be expecting us to do what Pirate teams have always done, work the ball in for the easy lay-up. I'd come at 'em with a surprise."

"Mr. Woodrow, tell me. If you were the coach of the Grand Haven Pirates, would you cut Nelson Woodrow, or would you keep him on the team?"

Woody hesitated again. Maybe with the right answer he had a chance to make the team after all. Maybe all his hopes rode on this answer. "I don't know whether *Woodrow Nelson* should be on this team. But I don't think that's the question that needs answering."

"And what would that question be?"

"Which of the players that have already been cut should be invited back?"

The coach turned to look Woody full in the face and leaned forward with his head cocked as if to say, "What did I hear you say?"

Woody charged on. "When you teach the set plays, and you only have eight men on the floor, the starters are only facing three opponents. It's easy to execute a play when you have five players and the other team has only three. If you've learned how to execute a play five-on-three, what have you learned? I believe you should have ten players on the floor so that the starters experience real life situations in practice and are better prepared for the game situations. Five-on-three is not real life."

The coach sat back in his chair. "What else do you know about basketball?"

Woody hesitated again. "I know that John Wooden once made 138 consecutive free throws playing for the Indianapolis Kautskys. I know that Edgar A. Dibble invented the fast break. I know that under the original rules of the game as proposed by Dr. Naismith, you couldn't dribble the ball. I know that..."

"Yes," Coach Coors interrupted him and stood up as he did. "Yes. Well, thank you for your time and your willingness to be...ah...candid, Mr. Woodrow. Or is it Mr. Nelson?"

"It's Nelson, sir. Woodrow Nelson, or Woody, as my friends call me, sir."

*****

Scooter was out of the shower and toweling off as Woody entered the locker room. "Well?"

"Well, what?" Woody wasn't in any mood to be cooperative. He would rather have been cut and had it over with than go through the third degree like that. He felt Coach Coors had trapped him into an impossible situation with no way out. If he didn't answer the questions, he was doomed. But Woody was sure his answers had doomed him even more than if he had refused to answer or given him some stupid answers. In effect he had told the coach that some of his time-tested methods could be improved. What had he done?

"You were in there a long time," said Scooter.

"You want to know if I got cut, right?"

Scooter nodded.

Woody sank to the bench in front of his locker. He

began attacking his shoe laces and sighed. “Not yet, Scoot. Not yet. The only good thing about it is I will probably only lose sleep one more night wondering and hoping.”

Scooter studied his buddy, who appeared to be in the depths of despair. “You know you haven’t given us the Question of the Day yet.”

Woody looked up. “The Question of the Day,” he replied, “is ‘why me?’”

*****

Back in his office, Coach Coors sat back in his chair with his hands folded behind his head and his feet up on the desk. He stared at the ceiling for a while, then he straightened up and got a pencil and a pad of paper out of the desk. He wrote “GAME 1 - ZEELAND” in big letters on the pad and underlined it. Then he made a list:

- fast, hard-working guards
- full-court press
- substitute often
- run them ragged

He skipped down a bit on the paper and wrote “GAME 2 - CHRISTIAN” and underlined it. Under Christian he wrote:

- shoot more
- control rebounds for easy lay-ups

He thought for a few more minutes. Then he wrote:

50% of 40 is greater than 75% of 20.

Then put the pad away, turned out the lights in the small office, and left for the day. But he didn't stop thinking about the small, intense young man who had invented the slam dunk and who knew that Edgar A. Dibble invented the fast break. Coach Coors had actually met Edgar A. Dibble and he didn't know that Dibble had invented the fast break. But he didn't doubt it was true. This Woodrow Nelson had just told him so, and Coors was inclined to believe it—and anything else he said.

Chapter 6

The Experiment

It was normal for Woody to be full of chatter at the dinner table, so his parents suspected something was wrong. By the time Sarah Nelson went back into the kitchen for second helpings, her boy hadn't said but two sentences.

Mr. Nelson tried to force the conversation. "How were things at school today?"

"Fine."

"How are you coming on your physics project, the static thing?"

"Static electricity. Haven't started yet."

"Weren't you supposed to do that with a partner?"

"Doolie Higgins."

"Is that Doctor Higgins's boy? I forget his name, you always calling him Doolie."

"Lester."

At that point his mother broke in. "Woody, honey, what's the matter? It's not like you to make us pry your day out of you. What is it? Did you get cut from the basketball..." she was interrupted by the ringing of the telephone, " ...team?" One short ring, then another. "I'll get it," she said as she put her napkin on the table and got up to go to the telephone.

"Hello? Yes, it is. Yes, I am. Certainly, I'll put him on." She turned and pointed the phone at Woody and said, "It's for you."

"Who is it?"

"I don't know. Not one of your friends or a voice I recognize," she answered holding the phone for him as he got up from the table.

"Hello?"

"Mr. Nelson, this is Coach Coors calling. I've been thinking over some of the things we talked about, and I think you'd make a real contribution to the basketball team. I'm calling to say that you'll find your name on the final roster when it's posted on the bulletin board in the morning. Just thought you'd like to know."

"Thank you, sir. Thank you very much. You won't regret this, sir, I promise."

"I'm sure you're right. Enjoy your evening."

"I will, sir. I will. And thanks for calling."

"You're welcome. Goodbye."

"Goodbye."

Woody hung up the phone. "Well, I'll be gol danged! I'll even be dang golled. Woodrow Peabody Nelson made the basketball team. And since there was only one Woodrow P. Nelson that tried out, it must be me! I thought my goose was cooked, but maybe I laid a golden egg instead!"

"Well done, my boy. That's great!" His father rose from the table to shake Woody's hand.

"Come here, you big lug." Sarah Nelson got up and held out her arms and gave him a big hug. "I know how badly you wanted it and how hard you worked for it. I'm so happy for you! Sit down, I'll get the dessert."

"What's this about your goose being cooked?" Mr. Nelson asked.

"Well, this afternoon after practice, the coach asked me to come into his office, and I thought he was going to tell me he was cutting me. Instead, he asked me a bunch of questions, and some of them were hard to answer."

*****

Shortly after dinner, Woody knocked on the front door of the Higgins residence. Dr. Higgins answered the door.

"Woody, it's you. Come on in. Lester is in the basement work room. He tells me you're going to make some sparks fly. Go on downstairs and join him."

Woody could hear President Roosevelt on the radio console in the Higgins's front room as he passed through. Dr. Higgins was apparently listening to the president's "fireside chat," a radio broadcast in which the president told the nation about the progress of the war. Woody went down the stairs to the basement where Doolie was leaning on a table looking over some instructions and drawings amidst a pile of materials.

"Hi, Woody. What'd Coors want with you after the practice? I had to get out of there and get my paper route started, so I couldn't wait for you to come out. He find out you were the one who taught us the basket dunking thing?"

"He pretty much knew it was me."

"You catch heck for that?"

"Naw, he just asked me a bunch of questions. It must have been some kind of test and I must have passed, 'cuz he called me tonight to tell me I made the team."

"You made the team? That's great. I'm happy for you..." Doolie hesitated. "Just don't play forward, okay? Don't be taking my spot or I'll have to lay a whuppin' on you."

"Somehow, I don't think you need to worry about that. Did you get all the stuff I told you we'd need for this project?"

"Most of it."

"Do you have the list?" Woody wanted to know.

"It's right here."

"Let's see. A glass jar. Ooh, that's a beauty. Where'd you get it?"

"My dad has all kinds of these to hold sterile things."

"You got metal foil, paraffin, cork stopper, hard rubber rod, copper wire, rabbit fur..." The "rabbit" fur was yellow striped—the same color as a mangy tomcat Woody had seen wandering around the neighborhood. "Funny looking rabbit fur. Whose cat?"

"I don't know what you're talking about. Besides, it's for the sake of science."

"A phonograph record, a piece of wool cloth, a cheap metal pie pan, a thumb tack, a pencil with an eraser, and a rubber door mat. Looks like it's all here. Good. Let's get busy. My idea is to do this in rough fashion to see if it works, then we can try different materials to improve it."

"You're the genius," Doolie offered. "Tell me what to do."

"Why don't you find the center of the pie pan and push the thumb tack up through the bottom. You may have to get it started with a small nail and a hammer."

Doolie took the pie pan over to a work bench and did some measuring. Then he pierced the pie pan with a sharp tool called a punch prick. After he pushed the point of the thumb tack up through the pan he brought it over to Woody.

"Now, you have some glue there somewhere. Take the pencil and put some glue on the bottom of the eraser and the point of the tack, then push the pencil, eraser first, down on the tack. Hold it upright until the glue dries," Woody directed. Meanwhile, Woody had placed the rubber mat flat on the work table and was holding the phonograph record with a pair of rubber-handled pliers and rubbing it with the "rabbit" fur. He could hear the small sparks snapping as the static electricity was generated.

"I think the glue is holding," Doolie announced.

"Good." Woody carefully laid the record on the rubber mat with the pliers and reached for the pie pan, picking it up with the pencil which was sticking upright in the center and had now become a handle. He placed the pie pan on the record.

"You understand what's going on here?" he asked Doolie.

"I have no idea," Doolie said.

"I'm transferring the static electricity I generated by rubbing the cat fur against the record onto the pie pan."

"I don't see anything happening."

"You will if you look under the pie pan."

Doolie bent down to look under the pie pan, but all he could see was the record. He reached over to lift up the pie pan. When his hand got close... ZAP!!!

"Yow!" he yelled, wringing his hand. "That hurt. And

I didn't even touch the pan. It got up and zapped me!"

"That was the cat getting the last laugh, Doolie."

"Very funny. Now what are we going to do?"

"We're going to collect this electricity in a jar," explained Woody. "Take this paraffin and melt it down over that burner there. You got an old pan you can use?"

"How about an old paint can?"

"If it's clean, it'll be fine."

Doolie set about melting the paraffin and Woody began molding part of the metal foil around the outside of the jar. He held it in place by wrapping copper wire tightly around the foil. He left some of the wire sticking out and bent it upward toward the top of the jar.

"The paraffin is melting," Doolie announced.

"Good," Woody said. "I think we're ready for it." With a brush he began coating the inside of the jar with the liquid paraffin. When he was finished, he pressed the rest of the foil against the paraffin, which acted like glue and held the foil to the inside of the jar.

"Almost finished. Now we need to push another piece of the copper wire through the cork stopper, like so, and bend it so it will touch the inner metal foil when we put the stopper on the jar. There. That should do it. That," Woody said holding the jar up, "is what is called a Leyden jar. Let's see how good this one works."

Woody charged up the record with the cat fur, put it

on the rubber mat, then laid the pie pan on the record. He then lifted the pie pan by the pencil and touched the pie pan to the wire sticking out of the cork stopper of the Leyden jar. He repeated the process several times.

"It's almost like I'm pouring electricity out of the pie pan into the jar," he observed.

"I don't see anything happening. How do you know if it's working?" Doolie asked.

"By bending the wire attached to the outside of the jar towards the wire sticking out of the top of the cork stopper," Woody said as he turned to recharge the pie pan. "Better do it with..."

ZAP!!! AAAH!!! CRASH!!!

"...the pliers." Woody said it too late. Doolie had bent the wire with his bare hand, and as the two wires neared each other, the jar sent out a considerable electrical charge. Both the shock and the surprise had thrown Doolie off his feet into a metal cabinet with a crash.

"Doolie, are you all right?" Woody hurried over to his partner who was flat on his back but still able to curse.

"Holy Mother of Mary and damn the ships at sea! What happened?" Doolie managed to sputter.

"Did I hear a crash? Is everything all right down there?" Dr. Higgins called from the top of the stairs.

"I'm not sure, Dr. Higgins. Maybe you better come

have a look," Woody called back.

"What happened?" Dr. Higgins asked as he came down the stairs.

"Doolie wanted to see if the Leyden jar we made really did have any electricity in it," Woody said, "and it works better than we thought."

"So that's it. Well, come on, Lester. Let's get you up. Volts won't kill you, just straighten the hair in your armpits. That's it. How are you feeling?"

"Wow! I felt that down to my toes. That's something. I was wondering if the voodoo magic Woody was working with the cat—er—rabbit fur was a joke or for real. I didn't get the wire very close, when pow! I got zapped."

Woody couldn't help but grin on the way home that night. The sight of big ol' Doolie Higgins laid full out on the basement floor with a very surprised look on his face kept replaying in Woody's mind. He was shocked, all right, Woody chuckled to himself. "Doolie," he said aloud, "you just got paid back for all the times you bullied me when I was a little kid and I wanted to beat up on you but I couldn't."

With a loud guffaw, Woody ran to a chunk of ice on the sidewalk and kicked it halfway down the block.

*****

True to Coach Coors's word, the following announcement was posted on the bulletin board the next morning:

THE FOLLOWING STUDENTS HAVE BEEN SELECTED TO REPRESENT THE PIRATES ON THE VARSITY BASKETBALL TEAM
FOR THE 1944-1945 SEASON:

Berilla, David
Denton, Carl
Greenberg, Samuel
Higgins, Lester
Merrill, Jacob
Nagtzaam, Donald
Nelson, Woodrow
Peters, Marvin
Secory, Gregory
Westerhoff, Eugene

—Coach Coors

As is customary, there will be an all-school pep assembly to introduce this year's team to the student body. Seventh hour will be excused at 2:30 for this purpose.

—E.V. Babcock,
Principal

Casey met Woody at the door of the school. "Congratulations, Woody. You made the basketball team. I'm so happy for you." She marched him up the steps and over to the bulletin board. Jake and Marv were looking at the list, as was Westie.

"Congratulations, Woody," Marv said. Jake nodded his head.

"One, two, three . . . eight, nine, ten." Woody counted the names on the list. There had been only nine on the last list. Now there was another name: Bub Denton. Bub was a smaller kid like Woody, scrappy and very fast.

It *was* a test in Coach Coors's office, decided Woody. But it appears he had passed it. And from Woody's perspective, so had Coach Coors.

*****

"Because of the pep assembly, our class time today is short, so let's come to attention and get started. Today we begin our chapter on the nature and properties of electricity," Mr. (Coach) Coors began the lecture in his seventh hour physics class. "The classic definition of electricity is the flow of electrons through a conductor from a negatively charged body to a positively charged body." He paused as the students wrote the definition in their notes.

"Man's first experience with electricity," he continued, "came from friction. The ancient Greeks noticed that bits of dust and straw could be attracted to a fleece that had been rubbed with amber. Our word *electricity* comes from *elektron*, which is the Greek word for amber.

"The first real experiments with electricity began around the middle of the 17th century. A German scientist by the name of Otto von Guericke noticed that sparks resembling lightning jumped from a spinning sulfur ball that he had rubbed with his hand. This was the first electricity-generating machine. By trial and error with different methods and materials, machines were developed that could generate sparks that traveled up to two feet.

"In the 18th century, machines were developed that did away with friction. These were called induction machines. Then, in the early 1800s a British scientist named James Wimshurst invented the most advanced induction static electricity machine, and it quickly became the standard for generating high voltage electricity for the purposes of scientific study.

"Wimshurst machines also had wide commercial use. In fact," continued Mr. Coors, "many of your homes had a Wimshurst machine in them up until a few years ago." Coors turned to a wall telephone that was lying on its back on his demonstration desk.

"You're all familiar with the wall telephone. It has a crank on the side, and when the user wished to ring up the central operator, he would turn this crank, sending an electrical signal to the operator."

Coors opened the phone box as he spoke. He pointed

to black iron horseshoe-shaped bars and a rotor which connected to the outside crank. The rotor, when turned through the magnetic field, generated an electrical charge.

"This, class, is a Wimshurst machine in its simplest form," Coors explained. "If you've ever been invited by a cruel older brother to hold on to the connectors while he turned the crank, you know how efficient these Wimshurst machines are in generating electrical charges."

A few students nodded and smiled.

"As efficient as a Wimshurst electricity machine is, however, if you stop turning the crank, the electricity generated by the machine is gone." The teacher turned the handle on the side of the telephone vigorously and as soon as the machine stopped turning, he touched the connecting knobs. "Nothing. Generating electricity was one thing. Capturing it or storing it was another," Coors continued.

"In 1745, Peter Van Masschenbroeck invented a device that stored electrical charges. Every student of physics since has been grateful that his device is named after the university where he worked, the University of Leyden in the Netherlands. It's called a Leyden jar, not a Van Masschenbroeck jar.

"I have a Leyden jar here." The teacher picked up

what appeared to be a silver thermos bottle. He had attached a wire to a connector at the top of the jar, another to a connector at the side of the jar. He touched the free ends of the wires together. "Nothing happens," he said.

"Now let's use the Wimshurst machine in the telephone to charge the jar." He attached the wire connected to the top of the Leyden jar to one of the connectors on the telephone. He connected the wire attached to the outside of the Leyden jar to another connector on the telephone. "Now we'll generate electricity by turning the crank on the telephone. The electricity we generate should flow through the wires to the jar." He turned the crank a few more turns and then disconnected the wires.

"Assuming all went well, we will have transferred the electricity we generated into the Leyden jar, where it is being stored. We can test our theory by touching the two wires connected to the jar." The teacher took one wire in each hand and slowly brought the two free ends together. When they were about a half an inch apart . . . ZAP! A spark jumped the gap between the two ends of the wire.

"The assignment I've given you to construct a Leyden jar out of materials you can find around your house is due the first day back from Christmas vacation. I'm sure your ingenuity and resourcefulness will produce some interesting results. Be careful. The discharge of a Leyden jar connected to 700 monks joined arm in arm is said to have lifted all of them off their feet."

Chapter 7

Whose Kiss?

The buzz in the gym grew louder as more and more of the students found their way onto the bleachers. By custom, the seniors sat in the best seats in the lower middle while the freshmen were relegated to the edges and upper tier. The members of the 1944-45 team had assembled in Coach Coors's physics room to be individually announced at the appropriate time.

The cheerleading squad had changed into their uniforms, which were new this year thanks to some very enterprising work by their mothers. Led by Casey's mom, the mothers had begged, borrowed, or stolen enough white yarn to knit sweaters and enough fabric to make the short pleated skirts popular for cheerleaders. No other girl could even think of wearing a skirt that exposed her knees, but for cheerleading it was considered a uniform. The cheerleading skirts were worn over the objection of Miss Grace Addison, the elderly English teacher and dean of women. From her point of view, one of the side effects of the war that was worse than rationing sugar was the permissiveness it brought. She was particularly horrified at the number of young women, some still in high school, who ran off to marry departing soldiers who had two-week furloughs before being shipped off to the far corners of the world to be shot at or shot up or worse. Since these romances were often begun in high school, Miss Addison worked to have the school adopt a PDA policy. There were to be no Public Displays of Affection on the school grounds. Since she was the only teacher with enough conviction in the rule to put teeth into it, couples were careful not to hold hands when and where Miss Addison was likely to catch them.

The rally began with the cheerleaders warming up the students.

WE ARE THE PIRATES, MIGHTY, MIGHTY PIRATES.
EVERYWHERE WE GO-O, PEOPLE WANT TO KNOW-O.
WHO WE ARE-ARE. SO WE TELL 'EM.

WE ARE THE PIRATES, MIGHTY, MIGHTY PIRATES.
EVERYWHERE WE GO-O, PEOPLE WANT TO KNOW-O.
WHO WE ARE-ARE. SO WE TELL 'EM.

WE ARE THE PIRATES, MIGHTY, MIGHTY PIRATES.
EVERYWHERE WE GO-O, PEOPLE WANT TO KNOW-O.
WHO WE ARE-ARE. SO WE TELL 'EM.

With each successive chorus, the cheerleaders urged the students to become louder until the gym windows around the balcony fairly rattled. Then Casey, their captain, signaled the end by two forward somersaults accompanied by stiff-legged jumps from her teammates. Then when the last echoes of that cheer died down, she alone addressed the students.

In a clear, ringing voice she cried, “Two Bits. Four Bits. Six Bits. A Dollar! If you’re for the Pirates, stand up and holler!” And as if they were connected, the students and the teaching staff rose as one and with one fist in the air roared, “YEAH!” The exception was Miss Addison, who registered her displeasure at the short skirts and display of legs by remaining seated. The look on her face said it all. Her attempts to promote modesty and decency were not working. She could tell by the amused look on Principal Babcock’s face that protests would be futile.

As the principal rose and walked a few steps to a podium near the front row of the bleachers, the crowd became quiet.

“As an educator,” he began, “and one who’s dedicated most of his now considerable adult life to the education of students, it is heartwarming to see you at least as excited about your basketball team as I know you all are about your studies.”

He paused as the students responded with a hearty laugh.

"We're here to introduce the young men who will represent us on the basketball courts for the 1944-1945 season. As one who has been following these fine court men since they were freshmen, I am excited about the possibility of winning another league championship, aren't you?"

The crowd responded with a roar of approval.

"I beg your pardon. I don't believe I heard you."

An even louder yell arose from the crowd.

"I take that as a yes," the principal said, beaming at his ability to rally the crowd. "To give us a preview of what we can expect from them this year, I've asked Coach Coors to say a few words and introduce the team to you. Coach Coors?"

The team was in the physics room. Woody and several others paced the floor. Others, like Dutchie and Scooter, were old hands at this and simply waited patiently. They could hear this year's cheerleading squad being introduced. Presently one of the cheerleaders, Lois Webber, who everyone called "Webb," stuck her head into the room. She had to stop giggling to speak to them.

"You guys should come out and stand by the gym door." She was grinning like the cat that swallowed the goldfish. "When Coach Coors calls your name, go out and stand behind him in front of the chairs that are set up. There's one for each of you. Wait until you're all introduced before sitting down," she tittered.

The team followed her out the door. Scooter and Woody were the last to follow. "What could be so funny?" Scooter whispered. "Webb's got a bad case of the grins and giggles."

"She acts guilty if you ask me," Woody observed.

One by one, Coach Coors announced the members of the team, pointing out the contributions of veteran players and the strengths of newcomers. Each player ran into the gym under an arch of cheerleaders' pompoms to the applause and cheers of the crowd.

When all the players had been introduced, Coach Coors told them to be seated and turned the program over to Mr. Thoma, a teacher in charge of the Saturday Night Club and many of the school's social activities.

Mr. Thoma carried an armful of black cloths. "Good afternoon, students. As you know, these players have won the honor of representing the school on the basketball team because of the skills they possess. Some of them are outstanding shooters, or good ball handlers. Some are fast, and some are tall. All of them are very perceptive young men.

"Well, the cheerleaders and I have designed a little test here, to show just how perceptive they really are.

Girls, please come forward."

Woody watched as the cheerleaders passed him. Some of them choked back giggles. What is going on here? he wondered.

"What we're going to do," Mr. Thoma continued, "is blindfold each member of the team. Girls, please take a blindfold and help me here.

"Now, we're going to ask one of these lovely cheerleaders to plant a kiss on a player..." The ooos, aaahs, and whistles that came from the crowd covered up the gasp that came from Miss Grace Addison.

"This is outrageous. We just can't have this," she hissed into the principal's ear.

"I quite agree, Miss Addison. Please take notes and we'll decide who to punish after the event. But for the moment, I'm rather enjoying it," the principal whispered back.

"... and see if that player can guess which lovely lady kissed him," Mr. Thoma finished when the crowd quieted down. "Are all the blindfolds in place? We'll start on the end here with David Berilla. David, if you'll stand up here..." Chappie slowly got to his feet. The students screamed and whooped it up again.

"Hands behind your back, David. That's it. Now lean forward just a bit."

The crowd quieted for a moment. What Chappie and

the rest of the blindfolded players didn't know was that in the midst of all the screaming and howling, their mothers had been brought into the gym to do the kissing. Mrs. Berilla quietly stepped forward and gave Chappie a kiss.

"Well, David, what's your guess? Who was the lovely lady that kissed you?" Mr. Thoma asked.

Chappie thought for a moment, shrugged his shoulders and finally said, "Abbie Smith?"

The students roared with laughter. "Would you like to see if you were right?" Mr. Thoma asked.

"Yes."

"Would it matter to you? All these young women are charming, don't you agree?"

"Well, no . . . er, yes, I mean . . ." and he just hung his head.

"Okay, David. You may take off your blindfold, but don't give any of your teammates any help. They need to guess for themselves."

When Chappie took off his blindfold and discovered he had just been kissed by his mother, his look of both astonishment and horror brought another roar from the crowd.

The principal leaned over to Miss Addison. "Maybe we ought to keep Mrs. Berilla after school for that public display of affection," he said with a grin.

"Marvin Peters, you're next," Mr. Thoma said. Marv sprang to his feet with enthusiasm, bringing another roar from the crowd.

"Okay, Marv, hands behind your back. Lean forward . . that's it . . . pucker up."

Mrs. Peters put her hands on Marv's shoulders, pulling him forward and kissing him good to the sheer delight of the students.

"Well, Marv, would you like to guess which one of our lovely ladies that might have been?"

"Ah . . ." Marv hesitated. "I think I know who it was, but I could be more certain if I had another kiss, just to be sure I was right." The students roared again.

Mrs. Peters didn't hesitate, and this time Marv kissed back. The crowd shouted and whistled.

"Well, Marv, you've had two tries. What's your guess?"

"Ginger Vanden Berg?"

The look on Marv's face when he took his blindfold off was even more amusing than Chappie's, and the students were loving it.

And so it went from player to player, each one guessing a cheerleader when in fact it was the player's mother. Scooter guessed his kiss came from Casey, because he didn't think Casey would allow another girl to kiss him. He also thought Casey might be a little sore if he guessed someone else.

Woody was the last player in the line. He was puzzled. He couldn't figure out what was so funny. He also remembered the cheerleaders were wearing white gym shoes, and yet the footsteps he heard on the wooden floor were made by street shoes.

There was also another problem. There were only six cheerleaders, and of the nine players ahead of him, no one got it right. What were the odds of that happening, Woody wondered. Each player had a one in six chance of guessing right, and there were nine wrong answers? The odds of that were 56 to 1, he figured.

"Woodrow, there have been all kinds of guesses and they've all been wrong. You're known to be a very perceptive student," continued Mr. Thoma, "so perhaps you can guess which of these pretty ladies will be kissing you." He felt someone touch his elbow and prod him to his feet. Woody wondered why Mr. Thoma kept calling them pretty ladies. They were just girls, after all.

"Hands behind your back, Woodrow. Pucker up now."

Woody was hoping it would be Evie TenCate as the lips pressed against his. Not too long, but long enough. He licked his lips and tasted lipstick. Which one of the girls wore lipstick? And he got a whiff of her perfume. It was Deep Secret, like his mother wore. Like his mother wore? Lipstick? Street shoes?

"Well, Woodrow, which one of these pretty ladies do you think planted that very tender kiss on you?"

Geeeeee willikers, Woody thought. It has to be. That's why the cheerleaders were tee-heeing and giggling like they were guilty of something. And ol' lady Addled-Daughter (as he called Miss Addison) wouldn't allow this much fun to be had with kissing.

"I think it's Sarah," Woody finally said in a soft, I'm-not-exactly-sure voice in case he was wrong.

"Sarah?" Mr. Thoma said as if he was puzzled. "We don't have a cheerleader named Sarah."

"My mother's name is Sarah," Woody said, more confident than ever he was right.

The crowd was quiet at first, until someone yelled, "Way to go, Woody!" Then applause filled the gym.

"Well, Woodrow, take off that blindfold and see," Mr. Thoma said, grateful Woodrow Nelson had been the last player kissed by his mother and not the first.

*****

"Leave it to Woody to figure it out," Casey said as she and Scooter walked hand in hand to the school the following Saturday night just behind Webb Webber and Dutchie. The topic of conversation was Friday's pep rally. "How'd he do it?"

"It was quite simple. If we all weren't so excited about getting smooched, we might have figured it out, too. He heard footsteps made by street shoes, and all the cheerleaders had gym shoes on. He tasted lipstick, and none of you wore lipstick. But the real thing that tipped him off was that he couldn't believe ol' Addled-Daughter, as he calls her, would allow that sort of hanky panky on her watch. So it had to be someone harmless, and then he recognized his mother's perfume."

"Addled daughter . . . who is that?" Webb wanted to know.

"Miss Addison," Scooter said. "Woody thinks she's addled, you know, touched in the head, and so he calls her Addled-Daughter instead of Addison."

"Doesn't he like her?" Casey wanted to know.

"I know he doesn't think she's too bright. As he put it, 'Remember, Scoot, half of all teachers are below average.'"

Dutchie laughed out loud. "As you said, Casey, leave it to Woody."

"Yes, leave it to Woody. But what about you, Gregory Secory? Do you really think I kiss like your mother?" Casey teased.

"Hey, I hadn't thought about that," Webb acknowledged turning to Dutchie. "Do you think I kiss like your mother? Huh? Do you, ya big oaf? And by the way, you seemed to be pretty eager for a kiss from just anyone who comes along."

Dutchie decided this was one of those moments when anything you said could get you in trouble, so he just grinned.

"And wipe that grin off'n your face."

Both boys were glad they were at the door of the gym.

The Saturday Night Club was the thing everyone did who didn't have to work on Saturday night. The seniors were more and more aware that the guns of war were closer in the future than they were in the distance. And while you couldn't see or hear them, those guns were like a magnetic force that propelled young people to every social event that took place. It drew them into relationships for fear this would be their last chance for romance before the draft letter came or the enlistment happened. So the Saturday Night Club events were well attended, even desperately so. There were games like ping pong, in which Webb and Dutchie were unbeatable at doubles. There was also dancing, sometimes to a live orchestra playing the big band hits of the day. When there was no live music, the 78 rpm records of Les Brown and his Band of Renown and Tommy Dorsey's Orchestra filled the gym.

The camaraderie at these events was strong. A girl didn't refuse to dance with a boy, even if she wasn't particularly fond of him. This might be his last dance before he left for the war. It was almost a patriotic duty to have at least one dance with a boy before a girl could complain that her feet hurt or she was too tired. So the bashful and the wall flowers were few. The romances that did exist were often intense. It was as if they were running out of time, and indeed, some of them were. Except they didn't know who. So everyone played hard and danced hard, and no one wanted the last dance to come to an end.

Dutchie and Webb won the mixed doubles ping pong tournament, again, but Dutchie lost to Jake Merrill in the singles. Scooter and Casey won the jitterbug contest and the free sodas at Presley's Drug Store. It would be a night to dream about—especially after the guns of war separated them all.

Chapter 8

The First Game

14 June 1944

Meine kostbarst Kinder:

Wie geht's mit Ihen... I ask myself this hourly... how goes it with you? At least the wonderful Blitzkrieg doesn't attack America. We wonder daily if the Americans will enter the war, but they have their own fish to fry in the Pacific Sea, no?

A blessing from God arrived last week when the few strawberry plants we have in our little garden bore fruit. A taste from heaven itself as we haven't any fresh fruit since . . . ach, I don't remember when.

It is very lonely here. All our friends have been , as they say, resettled to God knows where, and I fear He is the only one who knows and is reluctant to tell. The synagogue is now a garage for the Gestapo motor cars. Such defamation causes one to wonder where God lives now. If he still lives.

How is my Samuel? Does he do well in his Hebrew lessons? I shouldn't ask.

Mama sends her love. What love she has left is for you and we speak of you daily. She won't hear me com-

plain of my arthritis because she fears my work making timepieces keeps us alive. The pay is good but the Deutchmarks are worthless as there is nothing to buy. What there is must come to us under the counter from friends who supply us at their peril, God be praised. I can't find another soul to fix my teeth, but as my grandfather said, "It's not so bad to lose your teeth if the food is rotten."

At this point Mr. Greenberg stopped reading the newly arrived letter from his father and looked around the table. The ticking of the clock reminded all of them of the possibility they wanted to forget—that Grandfather Greenberg might be making timing devices for the Nazis.

Mr. Greenberg broke the silence. "As I recall, in his last letter he wrote, 'As my grandfather used to say, It's not so bad to lose your teeth if there is no food.' What is he trying to tell us?" Mr. Greenberg shook his head and continued reading.

The war is everywhere. Little children ride around on the anti-aircraft guns like carousels, and sadly it's the only carousel to ride.

I must go as my hands tire quickly these days. May the God of Israel continue to keep us all in His hands. Shalom."

Samuel looked at his grandfather's letter. The envelope looked as if someone had carried it around for a long time or for a long way. It was postmarked in the Netherlands again, like the last one they had received. It occurred to Samuel that his grandparents might not even be alive.

"Do you think Grandfather is making bombs, Papa?" Samuel asked.

"Hush, Samuel. It is dangerous to speak of," Mr. Greenberg warned.

"Why? The Germans can't touch us here," Samuel said.

"It's not the Germans we must worry about."

Samuel was puzzled. "Who then?"

"The Americans," Mr. Greenberg whispered.

Samuel just knitted his brow into a question.

"Do you want to answer the questions of the government policeman when he comes and asks you if it's true that the bomb that landed in New York was made by your grandfather?" Mr. Greenberg's voice was tight with fear.

"Isaac," Nettie Abrams said quietly. "This is America. We have done nothing wrong. We have nothing to fear. There are laws here."

"America is at war, Nettie. The rules are different in such times. Laws will be broken or new laws made if it serves the Yankees' purpose. Are there not thousands of U.S. citizens in concentration camps in the western states? They are U.S. citizens who happen to be Japanese. They look like the enemy. Hitler is not the only one who finds 'solutions' to undesirable citizens. Do you think the authorities would blink an eye before finding a 'solution' to the relatives of people who might enable the Third Reich to bomb American cities?"

"This is a Christian nation. It can't happen here. Our neighbors are good people. They wouldn't let it happen." Aunt Nettie said it as if she believed it.

"Germany is a Christian nation as well. Where were the good Christian neighbors on *Kristallnacht*, the Night of Broken Glass?" Mr. Greenberg's voice was intense. "Nettie, don't you remember hearing of the November nights in 1938 when gangs of Nazi youth roamed through Jewish neighborhoods all over Germany breaking windows of Jewish businesses and homes, burning synagogues, and looting? A hundred of our synagogues were damaged and thousands of our businesses were destroyed. Some 26,000 Jews were arrested and 'resettled' to Poland. Many were attacked and 91 were beaten to death. Where were the Christian neighbors then?"

Mr. Greenberg paused and looked away for a moment as if to focus his rage away from his family. "Don't say it couldn't happen here, Nettie. If it needs to happen for the preservation of the State, or what some madman thinks is the preservation of the State, it will happen here. Our American friends are not gods. They're human and such is the human condition."

The rest of the Greenbergs and Nettie Abrams sat around the table and said nothing. Samuel wiped his palms on his pants to remove the sweat and tried usuccessfully to swallow the lump in his throat.

*****

The mood at the Secory home was not much better. The newspapers were full of stories of a large-scale German counter attack in Luxembourg that had succeeded in recapturing some of the territory the Allies had liberated. Some called it the fiercest fighting of the ETO. The family was almost certain Rich Nagtzaam was in the middle of it. They hadn't heard from him for almost a week. The waiting seemed to fill the house like smoke fills a room. You could wave it away, but more just took its place.

The newspaper that day also reported that Sgt. Basil Corbett of the Third Army was missing in action. This only increased everyone's anxiety about Rich, since he and Basil were friends. The Nagtzaams and the Secorys thought of little else. Winifred thought of nothing else. She was picking at her dinner.

It was Merrill Secory who tried to maintain some form of normalcy. "So, Scooter, you have your first game tomorrow night. How does the season look?"

"We'll be good, Gramps. Real good. By the way, with the gas rationing the school can't let the team take the bus. We have to go by car. Can you take a car full?"

"Where's the game?

"Zeeland. We got Dutchie's pa's car. He's got gas because of his business. Doolie's dad has unlimited gas because he's a doctor. Coach Coors can get some gas from the school. But that's only three cars and we need five. Maybe Marvin Peters's dad can drive, but we're not sure on that one. If you could take the Packard . . . ."

"Wouldn't it be more economical to collect some ration books and buy enough gas for a school bus?" Ruth Secory asked the obvious question.

"It's a felony to transfer coupon books, m'dear. Up to ten years in the hoosgow and a $10,000 fine. I read just the other day the feds are camped out at the Straits of Mackinac to check the ration books of duck hunters going to the Upper Peninsula. They're serious about this."

"I know, but it's certainly less gas for one bus to go to Zeeland than five cars."

"You're absolutely right, but rules is rules. There would be five of us committing a felony, not to mention

Mr. Poel down at the gas station. And do you think for a moment there isn't a Widow Bach here and there who would turn us in?"

"Who'd squeal, Gramps? How would she find out?"

"How does that woman find out about anything? I'm not saying she'd run to the cops, but are you willing to bet a felony record that she'd not breath a word of it to a living soul?"

"She's a good lady with a good heart, and I'll not have us speaking ill of her." Scooter's mother stood up for the elderly woman who was the undisputed neighborhood queen of gossip and homespun wisdom. "She's done a lot of good for us over the years," she added, referring mainly to the time when her homemade remedy cleared up an infection Scooter had developed.

"The question is, can I drive a car full, Scooter? You can tell your Coach Coors I'd be delighted." It would be a nice diversion from sitting in his chair and waiting.

*****

Basketball practice that week was unlike any that Dutchie, Scooter, or any other veteran player could remember. Coach Coors put all the big tall guys on one team and all the smaller, faster guys on the other.

"The object this week is to learn how to execute an effective full-court press and at the same time how to break one," the coach explained.

Coors put the team to work. Five of them, Team A, worked to drive the ball down the court to the basket. The defending players, Team B, practiced a full-court press, playing very tight to Team A players, or "pressing" them. The goal of Team B was not only to prevent their opponents from getting the ball inbound to score, but also to frustrate them and provoke them into making mistakes that would give Team B the ball.

Learning how to execute a full-court press was physically demanding, and at the end of the practice the players were exhausted. It was Dutchie who expressed it for the rest of them.

"I have never practiced this hard as long as I've played for Coors. What happened to the good old days when we would just work on the plays? My feet are killing me."

"Mine, too," Bergie said. "I think I'm getting a blister. But if Zeeland throws a full-court press at us, I think they'll be sorry."

I don't think they'll be the ones throwing a full-court press, Woody thought. He thought he knew why they were practicing against the full-court press, and it wasn't because of anything Zeeland was planning to do to them.

"I wonder how Coors knows what Zeeland is going to throw at us?" Marv Peters wondered. "They haven't played any games yet, have they?"

"That's a good wonder. He must know something we don't. He ran us ragged, especially you little guys. You were all over the court," Scooter said. None of them had made a move to get out of their basketball gear. They were just sitting on the benches in front of their lockers trying to regain some of their energy.

"Speaking of wondering, what do you wonder today, Woody? We could use something to think about besides our aching feet," Bergie said.

Woody was as tired as any of them. He sat bent over with his hands folded and his arms resting on his knees wondering if playing on the basketball team was worth the effort he had just expended. But it was time for something to distract them all from thinking about how tired they were and how their feet ached.

"I was wondering why the word *abbreviation* is so long."

*****

The ride to Zeeland seem to take forever as the little convoy carrying the basketball team made its way along country roads. It was the first game of the season for everyone, and the first game ever for Woody. And he couldn't wait to see what Coach Coors had up his sleeve for Zeeland. He hoped beyond believing that if Grand Harbor was fortunate enough to get a big lead, he might have the chance to get a few minutes of playing time himself. But he didn't count on it. He worried that despite making the basketball team, he might never have the chance to get his uniform sweaty.

*****

"Gentlemen," Coach Coors addressed the team in the locker room before warm ups, "I've been told Zeeland is a good team. They've got a lot of height on us, and if they're disciplined and can shoot the ball, we may be in for a tussle tonight. We'll start Greenburg at center, Nagtzaam and Higgins at the forwards and Secory and Peters at the guards. But if I can see that our starters aren't prevailing, I'm thinking we'll spring the full-court press we've been working on these past practices. So you subs—Merrill, Nelson, Berilla and Denton—keep your heads in the game. We may have to throw you in there sooner than you think. If we do press 'em, we're going to substitute often to keep fresh legs. Now, let's remember who we are and the school and families we represent and acquit ourselves well. Let's go, gentlemen."

A few minutes into the game, Woody could see the Pirates were going to be in trouble. The Zeeland players averaged two or three inches taller than the Pirates, and their center was a hulk of a guy they called "Bruiser." Bergie was a better player but Bruiser was like a tank under the backboards, not allowing Bergie anywhere near it. Woody looked at Bruiser's basketball shoes. About size 17EEE, he guessed. Not exactly agile, Woody thought. He moves like a rhinoceros.

Six minutes into the game, the Pirates were behind 10-2. Zeeland fans were going crazy, and Coach Coors signaled to Scooter to call time.

"Everyone in the huddle," the coach commanded. When everyone had gathered around, Coors said, "We're going to switch to Plan B. Berilla, Nelson, Denton, you go in for Higgins, Secory, and Greenberg. Nagtzaam, you play forward and Peters, you move to forward opposite Nagtzaam. We'll play two men low and you guards show us what you can do on the press. Couple of turnovers and we're right back into it. Nagtzaam and Peters, if you do get the ball down low, I want you to drive to the basket. Maybe we can get their big ape to commit some fouls. All set now, any questions? Let's go."

Woody did have a question, and it could have been a Question of the Day. What was he doing here, a snip of a kid among these giants? He guessed it was proof of the old saying "Be careful what you wish for."

Well, he had wished for it, and now was his chance. What had Scooter said? "Play within yourself." That's what he'd do. Play within himself . . . if he could just get his heart out of his throat and his legs and arms working.

The Pirates took the ball out of bounds after the time out. Woody passed it to Chappie, who dished it off to Jake. Jake dribbled it toward the basket and bounce-passed it to Dutchie. When Bruiser lumbered out to guard him, Dutchie gave him a head fake toward the middle of the court, then whirled and drove to the basket. Bruiser was caught off guard, and when he changed directions to prevent Dutchie from going to the basket, he moved into Dutchie. The whistle blew, sending Dutchie to the free-throw line. Two underhand free throw shots later, the Zeeland lead was cut to 10-4.

Then the trap was sprung. All but two of the Zeeland players turned to trot up the floor, and Woody and Jake were all over the only player left to take the inbound pass. The three seconds allowed to get the ball into play passed too quickly, and the ref blew his whistle—Grand Harbor ball!

Marv made an easy lay-up off the inbound pass, 10-6. The Zeelanders caught on to the full-court press but were confused. They hadn't expected it and weren't prepared. The resulting confusion caused a player inbounding the ball to make a bad pass. Bub intercepted and made another easy lay-up to make the score 10-8.

When the Zeeland guard took the ball out of bounds

this time, he was a little more cautious. He managed to get the ball inbounded safely, but when that player turned to dribble up the court, he ran smack into Chappie and drew a foul. Chappie missed the free throw, but Dutchie put the rebound up and in to tie the game at 10 all.

At this point, the Zeeland fans were making so much silence you could hear the Zeeland coach ask one of his players to call for a time out.

*****

The ride home went very fast. If there were any tired legs or sore feet, no one complained.They felt only deep satisfaction from going up against a very good team and winning. Woody was the most satisfied of all. He had played about a third of the game, which was a third more than he expected. He had scored, but that was not what was replaying in his mind. About halfway through the second quarter, when the Pirates had taken an 18-14 lead, Coach Coors had looked right at Woody and winked. The feeling at that moment was far more satisfying than kissing your mother and guessing who she was or being able to do math problems in your head. In fact, it wasn't even close.

Chapter 9

How Does God Decide?

It was Saturday and Winifred was standing at the door waiting for the mailman when the letter came. It was very, very soiled, as if it had been dropped in a mud puddle.

December 2, 1944
Somewhere in the ETO

To my darling wife:

As you can see from this letter, there is mud, mud and more mud. I am not kidding, there is up to 7 inches of mud on the roads and nearly 500 German vehicles were stalled over the last five miles making it difficult to move an army. But we're making progress. For a time our company command post was in a small CENSORED *village. We were ahead of the advancing troops as artillery spotters, and we set up in one of five houses around a small town square. There were about 15 of us in this house when we heard rumbling on the road leading into the town square from the east. Much to our horror, two Kraut armored personnel carriers and a Panzer tank rolled into town. We all hit the floor. The tank turned its main gun in a circle and stopped it right at the window under which I had flattened myself. I could see the muzzle less than ten feet away from me. I guess they believed we had not advanced this far, because they turned around and left without so much as getting out of their Kubelwagons—those motorcycles with the side cars they favor.*

Let me tell you, the hair is still standing up on the back of my neck, and there was a line to use the bathroom after that—too late for some. The CO's aide was on the floor next to me and his hair has now turned totally white from the terror of staring down the barrel of a German Tiger tank. They don't fire the kind of bullet you can try to catch with you teeth.

Say hello to our neighbors two doors to the north. He's such a great guy and I look forward to hearing his great lines when I get home. Just got the word we have to move out, so this is all for right now.

I miss you so very much. Say hello to everyone. I think of you all every day. God bless you and keep me until we meet again. I love you so very much.

Rich

They had all gathered around as Winifred read the letter. No one made a sound. When she finished her hands were shaking.

"He had a close call, but he's safe," she said.

Ruth gave her sister a hug, and then the tears came from both of them. Then Winnie went up the stairs to her room and they heard the door quietly click shut.

Grandfather Secory had taken the letter from her and was now at the dining room table. He took out a big map of Germany. He laid the yardstick on the 49th parallel, moved it just a bit higher, and stretched the string along the seventh longitudinal line.

"What do you think, Scoot?" he asked.

"Saarlautern."

"I think so, too. But I think there's more. Who lives two doors to the north?"

"Mr. Svensen," Scooter answered.

"Do you know his first name?"

"No, I've always called him Mr. Svensen."

"It's Siggy, short for Siegfried. Our Rich is at the Siegfried line," the old man said without any emotion. "Put in the dot and draw the lines Scoot. I'm going to get the newspapers from around the first of December."

While his grandfather rummaged through a stack of newspapers he kept in his den, Scooter drew a dot with a red pencil on the German town on the Saar River named Saarlautern and connected the dot to the last one.

One thing was unmistakable: the red line was extending farther and farther from the beaches of Normandy on the west coast of France. The Third Army had moved through France and were now into Germany. Scooter wondered if there was going to be any war to fight when he got out of school. He hoped there would be.

"Here we are," the old man said as he returned to the dining room table. He laid down several newspapers. The top one was dated December 5, 1944, and its headline read:

PATTON'S ARMY DENTS SIEGFRIED LINE

Pass Saarlautern as Bridgehead Is Widened on Saar

Lt. Gen. George S. Patton's infantry drove completely through Saarlautern, second city of the German Saar, today and hammered deep into the Siegfried line defenses as tanks and troops were hurled into the expanding bridgehead across the Saar river...

"Gramps, what's so scary about a gun that's only five inches long?" Russell wanted to know. He had stopped playing with his baseball cards long enough to come over and look at the map.

"Russell, when Uncle Rich says a five-inch barrel, he means the hole in the end of the barrel is five inches wide. It's not like the barrel of our .22 rifle that you could stick a kitchen match into." He made a fist. "A man could put his whole arm into a barrel that size. It shoots a shell that weighs about 15 pounds, and if it hit a house as big as ours, it would reduce it to rubble."

"Jeesh! Almost makes my hair turn white thinking about it," Russell announced and then went back to playing with his collection of baseball cards. He was proud of the collection. Not only did he have the 1939, 1940, and 1941 cards of both Ted Williams and Joe DiMaggio, he also had many of the first baseball cards printed. He had Ty Cobb and Cy Young and Sherry Magee and some lesser known players like Pie Trainer and Honus Wagner. His grandfather had collected them in the days when he had smoked Piedmont cigarettes.

Russell's father had treasured the cards, and then Scooter had played with them by the hour. Now they helped Russell pass a snowy Saturday. They had always been stored in old cigar boxes, until recently when Russell mounted most of them in two photograph albums to keep them nice. But there was no adding new cards. Due to the war and the need for paper, card production had stopped in 1941.

Scooter read some of the papers his grandfather had brought to the table, catching up on news of the war he had missed. One story in the December 2 paper caught his eye:

Ensign Jacobson Swam 18 Hours

Clung to Coral Reefs of Jap-Held Islands for Days

Ensign A. E. (Al) Jacobson's escape from the submarine *U.S. Flier*, which was sunk in the Pacific war zone, is an epic of this war as he and seven others are the only known men in the service to have come back alive from a lost sub.

Not only did he escape from death aboard the ship, but he and the others endured grueling hours in the sea. The first 18 hours after their sub went down, he and seven others swam continuously before they found and dared to crawl up on a coral reef. The eight men clung to the reef for days enduring starvation and lack of fresh water, constant menace from Japanese patrols from land and air in the Jap infested islands, sunburn, and infection from the live coral reefs.

Ensign Jacobson along with 16 others were on the bridge when his ship was sunk...
"One by one," he said, "9 of the 17 were forced to give up. There were no calls for help, no word spoken as these brave men realized they were near

the end. They turned away from their fellows and died like Americans."

The story went on to tell of the sailors' ordeal as they made their way onto an island, drank coconut milk, trekked through the jungle in bare feet, were found and hidden by natives, and finally were rescued by American forces with nothing but their undershorts.

The article closed with this paragraph:

> After the men had recuperated in a rest camp in Australia, Ensign Jacobson was flown back to San Francisco. It was here the young man replenished his wardrobe, but he brought home the historic "shorts" and his mother says she shall preserve them for posterity together with the story of her son's miraculous escape.

Scooter's reading was interrupted by a knock at their back door. Before he could see who was calling, he heard "Yoohoo, anyone home?" It was the familiar voice of the Widow Bach. She was wheezing from her walk across the street and sunk into a chair in the kitchen to catch her breath.

"I brought you a batch of my apple pandowdy. Baked an extry one. Starting on my Christmas bakin' early, and I know how you like my pandowdy. Did you hear about the La Penna boy? He's the one shot down over Germany. Well, his mother got a letter from another flier who saw him parachute out of the plane safely. So they think he's a war prisoner. Least wise that's not as bad as being dead. I hear tell she's gone sick to grief over it. And who can blame her? This war business is no business. If the ones doin' the deciding had to do the fightin' there'd be no war, I always say.

"I also heard tell this morning that the Hornstra boy is missing in action in Italy. You know the Hornstras, Merrill. Them's the ones where I got my last batch of Leghorns. Best layin' chickens I ever had, too, if you ask me. What do you hear from the Nagtzaam boy? Is he all right? Ach, when I think of what those boys go through. Just count your lucky stars you're not over there getting shot at, young man," she said, addressing Scooter. "Maybe this thing will be over with before you have to go. I just hope they get this Hitler fella and give him what he's got coming to him."

At that moment Ruth Secory entered the kitchen. The Widow Bach didn't miss a beat. "Ah, Ruthie dear, brought you a plate of my pandowdy—apple this time. Baked an extry one. Starting on my Christmas bakin' early and I know how you like my pandowdy. Did you hear about the La Penna boy? He's the one shot down over Germany . . . ."

By the time the old woman was beginning her story for the second time, Russell had retreated to his baseball cards with a plate of the apple dessert, and Scooter excused himself to answer a knock at the front door. It was Bergie come to work on the physics project.

"If you can put up with the Widow Bach's chatter, there's some really good apple pandowdy in the kitchen," Scooter advised.

"Nah. Not hungry."

"You not hungry? Who are you and what are you doing in Samuel Greenberg's body?" Scooter asked good naturedly.

"Well, okay. Just a little." They detoured to the kitchen.

"Well, the Greenberg boy." The Widow Bach geared herself up for another appreciative audience. "Have some of my pandowdy. Baked an extry one. Starting on my Christmas bakin' early. Did you hear about the La Penna boy? He's the one shot down over Germany . . . ."

"That woman could talk the bark off'n a tree," Scooter said after they had escaped to his bedroom. "Aren't you going to eat your pandowdy?" he asked.

"Really not hungry."

Scooter looked at his friend. He suddenly realized Bergie hadn't been himself for a few days. "What's wrong?"

The lanky Jewish boy with the dark hair just sat on the edge of Scooter's desk and shrugged.

"Is it your grandparents? Have you heard from them?"

Bergie's no didn't convince either of them.

"Scoot, you gotta promise not to tell a soul," begged Bergie.

"I haven't told anyone about your grandfather so far, have I?"

"But this could be real serious."

"I promise. Is 'cross my heart and hope to die' enough, or do you need me to sign my name in my own blood?"

"This ain't funny, Scoot. My dad thinks they might come and take us away."

"What? What for? Who's 'they'? Where would they take you?"

"He says the government has sent lots of Japanese-Americans to concentration camps, and if they find out my grandfather is making timing devices, they'd come and take us away, too."

"Bergie, they won't let you fight in Germany because you were born there, but no one's coming after you because of what your grandfather's being forced to do for Hitler. That's crazy."

"Is it true that the government put Japanese-Americans in concentration camps?"

"I haven't heard about that. I did hear tell of a prisoner of war camp for German soldiers somewheres near here—like in Fremont or something. But come after you? Where'd he get such an idea?" asked Scooter.

"He's got me really scared. Scared for my grandfather and scared for us. You know, Hitler almost got us once. We got out by the skin of our teeth in '36 when we came here."

There was a pause. Scooter didn't know what to say to his friend. Then he cleared his throat and said, "Well, Hitler or no Hitler, we should get busy on our Leyden jar. Doolie said the one he and Woody made knocked him flat on his butt. I don't want to lose to those two. Eat your pandowdy so's we can get started."

*****

"You boys know it's Christmas soon and I don't think I have a Christmas wish list from either of my boys," Ruth Secory was cutting apple pandowdy for their dessert after the Saturday evening meal. "Who wants a slice of cheese on their pandowdy?"

"Russell, what would you like Santa to bring you?" Grandfather Secory asked.

"I hope Santa remembers I'd like another photo album for my baseball cards. I also want a Boeing B-17 Flying Fortress Bomber model airplane kit, but I'd take a P-38 Lockheed Lightning Fighter. That's what Scooter wants to fly, right Scoot?"

Scooter squirmed in his seat. He knew his mother wanted no talk of his participation in the war, so he just nodded his head.

"What's on your wish list, Scooter?" his father wanted to know.

What Scooter really wanted was a wrist watch, one with enough features to qualify as an aviator's watch. It needed a sweep second hand and possibly a stop watch feature and a tachometer feature—one that measures speed on a fixed course. But to go into detail would only upset his mother.

"A watch would be nice," he replied. "But I could also use a new pair of basketball shoes."

"We could also use a new basketball. We can't keep the laces tight on our old one," Russell remembered.

"If Santa looks at his list and checks it twice, will he find you've been naughty, or will he find you've been nice? Hmm?" Grandfather Secory peered over the glasses perched atop his nose.

"I'd say it's nip and tuck on that issue," Scooter's father said without looking up from his dessert.

*****

Sunday morning dawned cold and bright. Scooter's mother had made fresh sticky buns that morning, and he had eaten one more than he should have. He was sitting in church with a full stomach, and there was a temptation to catch a little nap during the minister's long prayer. But since his family had been selected to light the Advent candles that week, they sat near the front under the watchful eyes of the minister and the choir, so best behavior was required, even during the prayers.

The minister prayed for the safety of each of the servicemen by name: Julian Hattan, Jr., in the Pacific, Rich Nagtzaam in Europe. Scooter wondered why the minister thought it necessary to remind God where Uncle Rich was. Maybe there were two Rich Nagtzaams and the other one was in the Pacific. Actually Rich was luckier than most because the minister at the Dutch Reformed Church where Rich was a member was probably praying for him, too. It was only because Winnie went to St. John's Episcopal with the rest of the Secorys that Rich got the benefit of two prayers. Scooter wondered if the number mattered.

The minister prayed for the president and his cabinet and for the generals and admirals of the army and navy and for "victory over the godless forces of darkness that would enslave people against their will and their evil masters." Prayers like this one were going up to heaven from all over America at that very moment and had gone up earlier that morning from pulpits in England, France and the rest of the Allied countries.

That got Scooter thinking. He wondered what the people in Germany were praying that Sunday morning. There were Christians in Germany. After all, Martin Luther was German and the Lutheran Church was traced back to him. What were the Lutheran ministers and the Catholic priests in Germany praying for that Sunday morning, and what were they calling the Allies?

If God was a supreme being somewhere out there who answered prayer, Scooter wondered, how did He decide whose prayers to answer? And if God could intervene and cause one side's prayers to be answered—if He did have that power—why didn't He intervene before things got nasty? He could have caused this Hitler creep to have a heart attack back in 1936 and saved the world a lot of grief.

It was easy for Scooter to see that God answered prayer in some cases. His Uncle Rich had stepped on a mine and it was a dud. Then there was the Panzer tank driver who didn't pull the trigger. It was easy to believe that those incidents were answers to Aunt Winnie's and his family's prayers for Rich's safekeeping. And if the La Penna kid did bail out safely, wasn't that an answer to his family's prayers? That's easy to explain,

Scooter thought.

But what about the nine guys that didn't make it to shore with Al Jacobson? Didn't their families pray for them? And what about the guys who didn't get killed even though there was no one praying for them?

How did God decide? This one lives, not that one; this country wins, not that one. Scooter was glad he wasn't God who had to decide, or a minister who had to explain the decisions when they went the wrong way.

As the service drew to a close, Scooter noticed a bulletin board of sorts that had the names of all the young men in the congregation who were in the service. They were the same fellas the minister had prayed for earlier. His name would be on that list soon. He ticked off the months on his fingers: January, February, March, April, May, and he would leave in June, maybe before if he passed the Air Corps test for aviator school. Five months, six at the most, and he would be in the service of his country. He couldn't wait.

Better start praying for the Krauts and the Japs, he thought. They'll be the ones needing the prayers when I get there.

Chapter 10

Was It a Dream or Was It Real?

If the members of the basketball team thought the previous week's practice was strange, Coach Coors absolutely confounded them the first practice after the Zeeland game.

"It was a great win against Zeeland. It was one of the best team efforts of any game I can remember coaching. We executed our press very well and that obviously caught them off guard and allowed us to prevail against a very formidable opponent. This week's opponent is no less formidable but in an entirely different way.

"Whereas Zeeland was big and tall, Grand Rapids Christian is small and fast. So we should be ready for two things. First, we should be ready to break their full-court press should they throw it at us. Second, we need to press the advantage we do have, and that's size and height."

The practice was spent drilling the forwards on how to box out the opponents to control rebounds and putting the ball back up for easy lay-ups. The guards attempted shots from farther out than any Coors team had been allowed to shoot in the past.

"Of course we want to make each shot if possible, but it's just as important to make sure the shot is close enough to rattle the rim and enable our guys to get the rebounds," was the coach's lesson.

"What did you think of that practice?" Scooter asked Dutchie and Bergie when they got to the locker room. "I don't remember ever being allowed to shoot much past the 15-foot line. Tonight Coors was telling me to take 20, 25 footers. What gives?"

"Beat's me," Dutchie replied. "All's I know is that if the man says we full-court press 'em, that's what I'll do. If the man wants me to rebound, that's what I'll do."

Bergie chimed in. "I can remember getting reamed out for taking a shot that rebounded. 'If there's a rebound, that means you've missed the shot and we can't win games by missing shots,'" Bergie said, mimicking Coach Coors. "How many times have we heard that in years past?"

"Makes you wonder," Jake observed. "Which makes me wonder—Woody, what are you wondering about today?"

Woody was wondering whether or not the strategy he outlined to Coach Coors about how to beat Christian was the reason for the change in the structure of the practices. But that would have to remain private.

"You've all seen pictures of these Jap kamikaze pilots? You know—the guys that deliberately try to fly their planes into our warships on suicide missions?" Woody asked the boys.

"Yeah," came in a chorus around him.

"I was wondering why those guys wear helmets."

There were snickers all around.

"We got a letter from my older brother," Marv Peters interjected. "He was one of 12,000 soldiers on a 14-ship convoy in the Pacific when one of those buggers came in right over the waves at them. He got in the middle of the convoy and flew back and forth, apparently picking and choosing which ship he was going to take out. All the guys were on deck with their hearts in their throats watching this Jap play roulette with their lives. They were under orders not to fire at him, because if the gunners missed, they might hit another ship.

"So, anyway, they were all on the rail waiting to see who was going to go for a swim. When the kamikaze pilot got to the end of the line of ships, one of the navy gunners finally had a clear shot and . . ." Marv held up two closed fists with his elbows at his sides and pumped them rapidly while imitating the sound of an anti-aircraft gun. "When he splashed the Jap, my brother said that 12,000 cheers went up. Then they arrested the gunner, and he's up for court-martial."

"A court-martial?"

"What for?"

"Should'a given him a medal."

"He disobeyed an order."

The court-martial of the gunner was the topic of conversation on the way home for most of them.

*****

Woody inhaled good smells from the kitchen when he got home that night.

"Smells good. What's the meat?"

"Grouse. Your grandfather went hunting this morning and got four of them. He offered to give us two if I would clean all of them. I made your favorite chicken casserole with them, the kind with the biscuit covering."

"How do you make a chicken casserole with grouse?"

"Smarty pants. Just for that you just get vegetables. No grouse for you," she said kiddingly.

"I'm not grousing at you," Woody protested. "No ma'm, not me. I'm too chicken."

"Okay, enough of your fowl mouth," she said with a grin. "How did practice go today, honey?" She mixed some biscuit dough.

"Fine, Mom. Just fine. But I won't be playing as

much next game."

"Really, honey? Why not?"

"Different game plan. It requires good perimeter shooters and big, tall rebounders, and I'm neither."

"What kind of a shooter?"

"A perimeter shooter. That's a guy who can make baskets from far out, around the perimeter of the space where the defenders play. There's problems with that, though."

"What sort of problems?" she asked as she placed the dough atop the casserole.

"Coach Coors wants us to shoot two-handed set shots. In order to do that you have to be quite a distance from the guy who's guarding you, or he can swat the ball down. I think you could shoot from closer in if you jumped and tried to shoot when you're high in the air. That way the guy couldn't block the shot."

"Can you do that?"

"I could, but in order to do that you almost have to balance the ball with one hand and shoot the ball with the other. Coach Coors would never allow that. He thinks you need two hands on the ball when you shoot and also, that your feet shouldn't leave the floor."

"Well, he is the coach and he's been very successful for a long time. Where did you ever come up with such an idea?"

"From dribbling. You don't dribble with two hands, why should you shoot with two hands? Any word on Uncle Lou?"

"No, nothing. I think I just heard the paperboy. Will you check it for news, honey?"

*****

"I have to tell you about something that happened to me today." Sarah was enjoying watching her husband and son start on their second helpings of the chicken-grouse casserole. "I was at the armory rolling bandages and Johanna Boven was there. I may have told you about her. She's the one who sometimes entertains us by reciting poetry or Shakespeare. She told us that her son has been wounded in the war."

"That would be Bob Boven, right? I don't remember reading about him getting wounded," Mr. Nelson said.

"That's just it. They haven't heard about it officially. But she says she was asleep a few nights ago and awoke to find herself transported—in her nightgown, mind you—to a field in Europe and saw a column of men walking toward her. She said there was a white dog walking with them and the dog stepped on a land mine. The huge explosion appeared to kill every one of the soldiers. She went closer and saw mangled bodies everywhere.

"Then she saw a monk in his cowl coming down the

road. The monk stopped and turned over one of the soldiers. As he did that, she saw the soldier's watch and recognized it as the one her mother had given to Bob. Her son was so badly wounded she hardly recognized him, but he was alive. The monk put Bob over his shoulder and carried him back down the road, and it was at that point Mrs. Boven realized he had no feet."

"Bob's feet had been blown away?"

"No, the monk had no feet."

Both Woody and his father had put their skeptical faces on.

"What did the monk look like?"

"She said she couldn't see his face."

"And you believe her?" Mr. Nelson was incredulous.

"I do, I really do," Mrs. Nelson insisted. "Mrs. Boven's a very smart woman and not one to be frivolous. If she said it happened that way, I believe her. And if you heard her tell the story, you'd believe her, too."

"Well, we'll know soon enough," Mr. Nelson didn't sound convinced.

"Mrs. Boven envisions that something happened and concludes that it did," Woody said. "But what if you could envision something happening, and that helped you make it happen?"

"What ever are you talking about?" asked Woody's

mother.

"Well, the Wright brothers envisioned that man could fly, and they envisioned a machine that could do it, right?"

"Right."

"If they hadn't envisioned it in the first place, it wouldn't have happened in the second place, right?"

"I suppose so," his mother agreed reluctantly.

"Well, I wonder if you would be a better shot in basketball if you could envision the ball going in an arc away from your hand and into the net."

"I can understand envisioning a thing, but I don't see how you can influence an action by envisioning it," his father offered.

"You mean you can't envision envisioning?" Woody asked mischievously.

"If you put it that way, no."

"I wonder . . ." he interrupted his own thoughts.

"I wonder if there's any wonder in your wondering," Mr. Nelson said with a twinkle in his voice, and they all laughed.

"No, I'm serious. In shooting a basketball, if you imagine the arc the ball has to take, and imagine it going in, and then try to duplicate that arc when you shoot . . ."

It was more than his mother could imagine.

*****

Johanna Boven's dream was also the topic of conversation at the Secory's supper table that evening. Like Sarah Nelson, Ruth had worked at the armory that afternoon and had heard Johanna tell her story. After Ruth related it to her family, she sensed Scooter was skeptical and quickly defended Mrs. Boven.

"I believe her. And if you heard her tell the story, you'd believe her, too."

"Oh, I believe her," Scooter countered. "I was making a delivery over in Spring Lake to Mr. Cashmere's sister. As I drove down Lake Street, I passed the Western Union delivery boy on his bike. I noticed him because, well, you know, those guys aren't delivering birth announcements. After I made the delivery and got back to the truck, the Western Union kid was still riding around like he was looking for an address. He asked me if I knew where a Mr. and Mrs. Harold Boven lived.

"I was about to tell him I didn't know the neighborhood when a lady came out on her front porch and asked if he was looking for the Bovens. He said he was. And this lady came off'n her porch and said, 'I've been expecting you.' We both must have had our mouths wide open, because after she took the telegram she turned to us and said, 'It's all right boys. He's not dead, just wounded.'"

"That's quite a story, both parts of it," Merrill Secory observed. "What do we make of stories like that?"

"That she's a witch?" Russell asked in all seriousness, but everyone else laughed at that.

"What do you think, Scooter?" the old man pressed.

"I don't know what to think. Nothing like that ever happened to me. But I'm not sure just because it didn't happen to me, it couldn't happen to someone else."

"I think it shows how strong the bond is between a mother and her children," was Scooter's mother's take on the story. "More meatloaf or scalloped potatoes, anyone? There's a little bit of each left."

"What do you think, Gramps?" Russell wanted to know.

"I admire the woman's courage."

"Courage?" Scooter's father asked.

"Yes, courage. If that had happened to you, would you have the courage to tell anyone and risk your friends and neighbors..." and at that the old man started drawing circles around his ear with his pointing finger just as the Widow Bach was known to do.

*****

Friday brought the last basketball game before the Christmas break. Practices had alternated throughout the week. One practice was drills for the forwards and centermen on boxing out the opponents to control the rebounds and shooting drills from the perimeter for the guards. The next day the team would practice working the ball in close for the high percentage shot.

Since it was the first home game of the season, everyone expected the gym to be packed with students and their families as well as interested townsfolk who were looking for some distraction from the war.

Woody saw Scooter and Dutchie walking toward the school with their gym bags in hand. "Hey, you guys. Wait up!" and he broke into a run to catch up.

Scooter was looking at him funny. "What's the matter? I got spaghetti sauce on my face or something?" Woody asked and his hand went up to wipe his mouth.

"Did you get your letter?"

"Letter? What letter?" Woody wanted to know as they started walking toward the school.

"A letter from the Army Air Corps."

"No, did you get one? What did it say?"

"We both got one," Scooter said, indicating Dutchie had gotten a letter too.

"Well, what did it say?" Woody asked.

"We got accepted."

"Gee," Woody paused only for a second before he said, "that's great, you guys. Congratulations." But in that second he concluded that the ones who didn't get a letter were rejected. So he wasn't able to hide the disappointment in his voice.

"Yours will probably be in the mail tomorrow, Woody." Dutchie sensed his friend's disappointment. "I can't imagine you failing a test that I can pass."

That's true, Woody admitted to himself. But Dutchie hadn't almost attacked the testing officer like he had. If and when the letter did come, he was sure the results would probably reflect the attack as well as the test scores.

As the players got into their uniforms, they laughed and talked against the background of the pep band warming up in the gym. All except for Woody. Scooter felt sorry for him. Woody was so smart and tried so hard. Who else was teaching himself German in case he was shot down behind enemy lines? Scooter didn't know whether to leave him alone with his thoughts or to try to cheer him up. He decided to try to be normal and asked, "Woody, what's the wonder for tonight?"

He was slower than usual to respond, Scooter thought. But finally Woody turned to Scooter and said, "I wonder if at first you don't succeed, should you try to be a paratrooper?" There were snickers around the locker room, and Woody seemed to brighten.

Just then Coach Coors entered. "Gentleman, we lost last year to what is essentially the same team we're going to play tonight. Last year we tried to work the ball in for the high percentage shot. That's what they'll be expecting this year. So I've decided to have you shoot more often from the perimeter. While I don't expect you to miss, if you do, our big forwards will control the back boards and we should be able to get some easy put-backs like we've practiced all week.

"We'll start Greenberg at center, Nagtzaam and Westerhoff at the forwards, and Peters and Secory at the guards. The rest of you keep your heads in the game. Just like last game, we may need to switch tactics, so be ready. Okay, let's go out there and get warmed up."

Woody could hardly believe the noise as they came out on the court. The pep band blared the school song, cheerleaders jumped and yelled, and the crowd was already on their feet screaming. There were banners hanging from the balcony, and Woody spotted his mom and dad in the second row. For a time he almost forgot about not getting an acceptance letter from the Army Air Corps. Almost.

Bergie won the tip-off and the Pirates took the ball down the court. Scooter dribbled to the perimeter and looked as if he were trying to get the ball in low. As he did, the Christian player stepped back a bit to cut off the expected pass. At that moment, Scooter set up and shot instead, banking the ball off the back board and in. Pirates 2, Christian 0.

Christian was fast and came up the court in a hurry. They had the Worst twins on their team—Joel and George—two outstanding players. They worked the ball around the perimeter and then moved it inside to their centerman, who tried a hook shot. Bergie didn't give him much room and jumped with him to block the shooter's view. The shot rattled the rim and bounced out. Dutchie came down with the rebound, and the Pirates took the ball up the court. This time it was the man guarding Marv Peters who stepped back, anticipating a pass, and instead Marv set up for the shot. Pirates 4, Christian 0.

The teams traded baskets for a few trips up and down the court. At the point when the score was 10-6, Dutchie got an easy put-back for two points. Christian's guards brought the ball up the court, but Scooter stole a sloppy pass, had an uncontested fast break, and made an easy lay-up. Pirates 14, Christian 6.

At this point, Christian's coach asked for a time out.

"Everybody in the huddle," Coach Coors commanded. "Listen up, fellas. So far, so good. Unless I miss my guess, he's telling his players not to collapse back to defend against the penetration passes. He going to tell them to come out more to contest the shots we're taking from the perimeter. So here's what I want you to do. If I'm right and their guards come out, I want you to go for the penetration passes. You all know how to work that to perfection. If they don't contest the shots from the perimeter, we go with what's been successful for us. Higgins, you report in for Westie—we may need a little more toughness down low. All set now? Any questions? Let's go."

The way he said it, Coach Coors didn't expect any questions. Woody had one for him, but it was answered when Coach Coors looked right at him and winked. The wink told Woody he was a bigger part of the team than anyone knew. The alternating strategies worked, and although Christian was able to keep the game close—largely because of the Worst twins—the final score was 32-26. The Pirates had two wins and no losses in the season when everyone went home for the Christmas break.

Chapter 11

Peace on Earth—Please

Field Marshal Gerd von Rundstedt, considered one of the most brilliant German field commanders, had under his command 23 German infantry and tank divisions—about 300,000 soldiers and their equipment as well as over 400 airplanes. They were preparing for a massive counteroffensive in the Ardennes Forest area of Luxembourg which was designed to drive the Allies back through Belgium to the North Sea. This battle would become one of the war's deadliest.

The American Third Army, which was under the command of General George S. Patton, had landed at Normandy on the western coast of France over a month after the initial landings by the Allied armies on D-Day, June 6, 1944. On the day it arrived, the Third Army began a campaign that would carry it east through Paris to the Saar region of Germany, and on to the German city of Koblenz by the war's end. Driving some of the finest fighting units of the German army out of France and back into their homeland was one of the most significant accomplishments of the Allied armies in the war.

On December 16, the Third Army was poised at the German border. The American First Army was to their north, having driven the Germans out of the Netherlands and Belgium. Both armies planned to continue their attack on the German homeland when General George S. Patton's intelligence officer told him the enemy to the north had gone on radio silence.

"What does that mean?" General Patton asked.

"When we go on radio silence it means we're going to attack. I suspect it's the same for them. I'd say they are planning a major counter-attack."

Patton hesitated for a moment, then said, "Right. We may have to pull the First Army out of a hole."

That very day von Rundstedt attacked with a combination of infantry soldiers, tanks, airplanes, and paratroopers dropped behind the Allied lines. His goal was to strike suddenly and hard at the weakest point of the Allied lines in the Ardennes forest region of Luxembourg. Here only three divisions of American troops (about 30,000 soldiers) held nearly 90 miles of front lines. If that line could be pierced, von Rundstedt believed he could capture Leige and Antwerp, the Allies' largest base and the seaport that supplied the American, British and Canadian armies. This would separate the Allied armies in Holland from the Allied armies in France. Von Rundstedt was betting that if a blitzkrieg (literally "lightning war") had worked earlier in the war, it could work again, and so he threw a huge army of 300,000 soldiers at the thin Allied lines.

In three days, the German army opened a breach in Allied lines 80 miles wide and 50 miles deep. But that's as far as the Germans got. They made a dent, or a bulge, in the Allied lines, but were unable to break through, thanks to the American forces, who were outnumbered ten to one. The battle in the Ardennes Forest region became known as the Battle of the Bulge.

The Germans attacked so swiftly that many American troops were trapped behind the advancing German army. An important army headquarters commanded by Brigadier General Anthony C. McAuliffe in the city of Bastogne was completely encircled. Somehow these troops had to be saved.

On December 19, General Dwight D. Eisenhower and his Allied generals met to decide a strategy to stop the German advance and counterattack. Eisenhower turned to General Patton and said, "George, you must stop your attack to the east and attack north to rescue Bastogne. How long before you can do it?"

Without any hesitation, Patton replied, "I can make a spoiling attack with three divisions in three days or a full-scale attack with six divisions in four."

"Now, George," Eisenhower chided, "don't be fatuous. I'm serious."

"So am I! I have three divisions now out of action and refitting, and if you let me go to the phone they'll be moving in an hour."

What Patton suggested seemed impossible. But the cocky general went to the map and outlined three possible plans. "Operation Nickel," an attack toward Bastogne to relieve the trapped troops in the headquarters there, was selected.

Patton strode to a telephone and asked to be put through to his command center. He waited for the connection and said, "This is General Patton. To whom am I speaking?"

"Tech Sergeant Richard Nagtzaam, sir."

"Sergeant Nagtzaam, put General Eddy on the line." General Patton paused. When he heard General Manton Eddy's voice he continued. "Manton? This is George. Get the 12th Corps ready to roll. Operation Nickel."

An army cannot simply start marching. Supply men worked around the clock to gather food, ammunition, fuel, clothes—62 tons of things needed to fight a war. But in a few short days, more that 130,000 vehicles had pushed northward to an unfamiliar front 150 miles away in an effort to get to Bastogne and bring relief to the trapped and freezing American troops.

Meanwhile, the German officer who commanded the

troops that surrounded Bastogne sent a truce envoy to meet with General McAuliffe, the American commander. The envoy hoped to get McAuliffe to surrender so that they could continue their advance toward Antwerp.

"The fortune of war is changing," read the surrender ultimatum from General Heinrich Frieherr von Luettwitz to the defenders of Bastogne. "There is only the possibility to save the encircled USA troops from total annihilation. That is, the honorable surrender of the encircled town!"

General McAuliffe's reply was very short. "Nuts!"

The German truce delegation did not seem to understand the general's snappy reply. The German army did not press their attack against the beleaguered Americans. McAuliffe radioed for reinforcements and planned a counterattack.

The weather was unfavorable for battle. Snow, ice, and sleet made the soldiers' lives miserable. Worse, the stormy weather made flying impossible, so the Allies' air superiority could not be used against the Germans. General Patton was a very religious man. He decided the only one who could help was, as he said, "The Good Lord." He directed all the chaplains to pray for good weather and ordered one army chaplain to publish a prayer for good weather. The prayer was printed on a small card and was issued to all units. On the reverse side of the card was a personal message from the general. The general followed this up with orders that wherever possible, every soldier should receive a hot turkey dinner on Christmas.

On December 23, the skies cleared and the weather remained perfect for six days. On the first day of clear weather, the Allied fighter planes flew 2,000 missions, swooping down to bomb German tanks and strafe enemy positions. There were 15,000 missions the second day. It was reported that the there were so many contrails in the sky, it looked as if the clouds had returned. The tide of the battle turned to the Allies. It was the best Christmas present the Allied soldiers could have had.

While General Patton attcked from the south, the First Army attacked from the north and the British Army advanced from the west. Their progress was speeded by the support from the fighter planes.

By December 26, the Third Army had made such progress that General Patton was able to approve a tank charge to Bastogne. By afternoon, the 37th Tank Battalion of the Fourth Armored Division broke through to Bastogne and made contact with the soldiers who had been trapped by the Germans.

The rescued troops and townspeople were overjoyed as they greeted the first American units. "They did everything but kiss us," recalled one of the officers of the liberating forces. "I felt like Santa Claus."

It took another 30 days to drive the German forces back over the Luxembourg border. By that time the cost in lives and equipment was staggering for both sides. In slightly less than six weeks, the Third Army lost 32,224 men—4,796 killed, 22,109 wounded, and 5,319 missing. In total, the Allied armies suffered over 76,000 casualties, the Germans over 81,000.

Miraculously, Tech Sergeant Rich Nagtzaam wasn't one of them.

*****

On Sunday, December 24, 1944, at the same time the battle was going on in the Ardennes Forest, the Sunday School Department of the St. John's Episcopal Church in Grand Harbor was putting on its annual Christmas program after the regular Sunday morning worship service. Woody and his family stayed to hear the program as did the Secorys.

There were nine children from Miss Trudy's four-year-old class, each with a letter spelling out C-H-I-R-S-T-S-M-A, until the teacher was able to get them in the right order to make C-H-R-I-S-T-M-A-S. Each child had a verse to say, starting with "C is for the Christ child" and ending with "S is for the stable where he lay." The girl with the M was so bashful she pulled her skirt up over her face to hide from the audience, so the precocious little boy with the A said her line—"M is for the Magi"—and his own line, "A is for the angels who sang 'Peace on Earth.'" The audience chortled, but the little girl's parents were not amused at the sight of her panties.

The five- and six-year-olds sang "Silent Night" in a whisper, as if they didn't want to waken the sleeping baby Jesus from the heavenly peace they were singing about. Woody wondered if it was appropriate to sing "Silent night, holy night. All is calm, all is bright" when, in fact, the night wasn't silent and all was not calm in the world.

A girl from Mrs. DeBoer's class recited the words to "Christmas Bells." The poignant words struck home forcefully as the girl recited the poem.

I heard the bells on Christmas Day
Their old, familiar carols play,
And wild and sweet
The words repeat
Of peace on earth, good-will to men!

And thought how, as the day had come,
The belfries of all Christendom
Had rolled along
The unbroken song
Of peace on earth, good-will to men!

Till, ringing, singing on its way,
The world revolved from night to day,
    A voice, a chime
    A chant sublime
Of peace on earth, good-will to men!

Then from each black, accursed mouth
The cannon thundered in the South,
    And with the sound
    The carols drowned
Of peace on earth, good-will to men!

It was as if an earthquake rent
The hearth-stones of a continent,
    And made forlorn
    The households born
Of peace on earth, good-will to men!

And in despair I bowed my head;
"There is no peace on earth," I said;
    "For hate is strong,
    And mocks the song
Of peace on earth, good-will to men!"

Then pealed the bells more loud and deep:
"God is not dead; nor doth he sleep!
    The Wrong shall fail,
    The Right prevail,
With peace on earth, good-will to men!"

Woody knew these words were written by Henry Wadsworth Longfellow during the Civil War, but they could not have been more relevant at that very moment. He felt his emotions rise and fall with the words, and when the girl finished, there was no applause, only silence. It was as if the audience in the small church offered the final words in a silent prayer: "Dear God, peace on earth—please."

After the rector thanked the participants, he wished everyone a very merry Christmas and dismissed the congregation. The Sunday school teachers passed out an orange and hard candy in small mesh Christmas stockings to each of their pupils, and everyone spilled out of the church into a snowy morning.

The words of "Christmas Bells" went with them. Some folks carried a bitterness in their hearts that couldn't be erased by the words of a poem. They had lost dear ones or had sons in harm's way. The Battle of the Buldge was raging in Luxembourg, and it wasn't going well. The words "For hate is strong, and mocks the song of peace on earth, good-will to men" went home with them.

Others carried hope in their hearts, remembering the next verse of the poem: "Then pealed the bells more loud and deep: 'God is not dead, nor doth he sleep! The Wrong shall fail, the Right prevail, with peace on earth, good-will to men!'"

To Scooter and Woody, the cry for "peace on earth" was heard as a call to arms. Neither could wait to get into the uniform of their country to help bring about that peace on earth, even if they had to cause a little "cannon thundering" to do it.

*****

Christmas morning dawned like a picture postcard. Large snowflakes were falling, making the world outside white and silent. After a breakfast of Ruth Secory's world famous sticky buns (Rich Nagtzaam was taking orders for them from his buddies in Europe) and hot chocolate with whipped cream, the Secorys gathered in the living room to exchange the gifts that had been waiting under their Christmas tree.

Russell got his B-17 Flying Fortress Bomber and the P-38 Lightning (just in case Scooter did get to fly it). Scooter opened a box from Grandfather Secory that he thought contained a basketball. At first he found a lot of crumpled up newspapers, but at the bottom he discovered a smaller box, also in Christmas wrap. When he opened it, there was the most beautiful watch he had ever seen! It had a brown leather band and a white face with five hands telling the seconds, minutes, hours—as well as a stopwatch hand and a telemeter hand. This was clearly an aviator's watch! Scooter turned it over in his hands and read the inscription: "MGkyiHhabyoew."

As he looked up to thank his grandfather and ask what the strange inscription meant, he noticed his mother staring out the window. Instantly he knew that words would only make things worse for her. His grandfather watched Scooter, and then nodded and winked.

Both understood that the meaning of the inscription would wait. The words "May God keep you in His hands and bear you on eagles' wings" would have been more than Mrs. Secory could bear.

Scooter was so proud of the watch, he couldn't wait to show his friends when they went tobogganing that afternoon at Mulligan's Hollow. Woody, Dutchie, and Bergie thought it was the cat's meow. To Scooter's dismay, Casey lacked the boys' enthusiasm. After he showed it to her, she wasn't her upbeat self. She even seemed to hold his hand tighter than usual.

Scooter wondered what it would take for the women in his life to understand that he had to go fight in the war. German warships in the harbor visible from where they were sledding at this very moment? Planes bombing Grand Harbor? The Greenbergs being carted off to a resettlement camp because they're Jewish, or the Widow Bach because she's a gypsy?

Casey was wondering why the people in Europe couldn't fight their own war. And so what if the Japanese wanted to have the Philippine Islands. That was no concern of hers. Why was Scooter so determined to go off and fight who knows who? Didn't he want to settle down, have a family, and grow old in Grand Harbor? She held his hand tightly, as if she could hold him back.

Chapter 12

Question of the Day

December 23, 1944
Somewhere in the ETO

To my darling wife:

I just met a general of the army. What a commanding figure he is. Three stars on his helmet and he carries a pearl-handled revolver as his side arm. He shook my hand and thanked me for my service to my country. I told him it was an honor to serve under him. He asked me where I was from and I told him a town about 110 miles north of Grand Rapids. He said he had been to Grand Rapids. After that meeting, I can tell you I was bulging with pride and had to battle not to hug him.

I had an opportunity for a promotion. The commanding officer (CO) of our company came and offered me a position as his aide. I told him I liked being a radio operator and would prefer to remain in that capacity. Also, we had no one else qualified to be a radio operator. He accepted that and found another man to take the job. That guy went from buck private to corporal in two minutes. That night the CO and his new aide went out to scout out the surrounding area.

They didn't come back.

You can imagine that I really like being a radio operator now and will continue to do that as long as I am able.

Christmas approaches and it makes being here in this terrible war even more horrible. From the looks of things, there won't be any heavenly hosts singing "Glory to God in the Highest" in this part of the world this year. But if things keep going and I get clean socks soon, I'll be home for Christmas—next year.

I miss you so very much. Say hello to everyone. I think of you all every day. God bless you and keep me until we meet again. I love you so very much and I miss you like a rocket's red glare.

Rich

"What do you make of it, Grandpa?" Scooter asked.

"Unless I miss my guess, he's met General Patton, and he's fighting in the Battle of the Bulge. He's in the Third Corps of the Third Army. That's the unit that's attacking Bastogne from the south and is 110 miles north of Metz, his last position. If I catch his meaning, there's a dreadful amount of bombing going on."

"The paper said it was the heaviest fighting of the war."

"Yes, it did," the old man said quietly. "We'll just have to hope and pray that this Patton fellow knows what he's doing and that Rich'll be okay. I suspect Rich has seen some of the V-1 rockets we've been reading about in the papers."

"That's what he means by the rocket's red glare?"

"I think so."

"We don't have any weapons like that, do we?" Scooter asked.

"No, we don't. I've read they are unreliable but really terrorize people. Apparently, they haven't perfected the guidance systems and timing devices so some of them go off course, and some of them blow up before they're supposed to. Some of them are just plain duds. From what I read, you can hear them coming from a long way off, and they scare the bejabbers out of folks. You stop whatever you're doing and listen. As long as you can hear them, you're safe. But when the engine stops, that's when they're supposed to come down, and you better be under cover. If they ever get the bugs out of them, they're gonna be devastating."

Timing devices. Scooter remembered the conversation with Bergie about his grandfather making timing devices for the Nazis. Was it possible that the grandfather of a kid that lived across the street and played center on the basketball team was making the timing devices for Hitler's V-1 rockets? And his Uncle Rich was seeing those rockets flying overhead? He could feel his jaw tense. He ground his teeth and looked at his aviator model watch. He wished he could be over there bombing the factory that made those rockets—whether Samuel Greenberg's grandfather was in that factory or not.

The front doorbell interrupted his thoughts. It was Bergie with a cardboard box under his arm. "I got most of the stuff we need for the Leyden jar," he said.

"Oh, yeah. I forgot we were going to work on that. Come on in." Scooter opened the door wide to let Bergie come in with his box. "I got the rest of the stuff in my room. Let's work up there."

Scooter had brought his grandfather's old hand-crank telephone down from the attic to use for generating an electrical charge. He fished under his bed for the rest of the stuff he had been saving for the project, as well as a pair of wire cutters and some other tools.

Scooter waved some metal foil he had salvaged from a shipping crate from Argentina. "No metal shortages in Argentina," he said, "but then they aren't fighting a war." The boys cut the foil into two three-inch strips and then faced the problem of affixing one of the strips to the inside of a pint Mason jar. They tried model airplane glue, but that wouldn't stick to the glass.

"What about rubber cement?" Bergie asked.

"I think we have some of that somewheres. I'll check

while you put the other strip of tin foil on the outside of the jar. I think if we strip the insulation off some of that wire and wrap it around the jar, it'll hold the foil in place," Scooter suggested. He returned with a jar of rubber cement just as Bergie was finishing wrapping the wire around the jar.

Bergie coated the inside of the jar and one side of the remaining strip of foil with rubber cement. When the cement dried, he fitted the foil to the inside of the jar and pressed out the wrinkles and bubbles as best he could.

Scooter had cut a round stopper that fit into the mouth of the jar out of some rubber tire patch material. He poked another strand of the wire though a hole he had made in the stopper and bent the wire so it came into contact with the foil on the inside of the jar. He left enough wire sticking out of the top so it could make contact with the wire wrapped around the side of the jar.

"There," Scooter said. "Let's see if this baby works."

With some additional wire the boys connected the terminals on the telephone to the wire on the side of the jar and the wire sticking out of the top of the jar.

"A couple of cranks?" Bergie asked.

"Just a couple," Scooter said tentatively.

Bergie turned the handle on the old wall telephone.

Scooter gingerly bent the insulated part of the wire toward the wire on the top of the jar. When it was about a quarter of an inch away—ZAP!—a blue spark jumped across the gap.

"Hey!" Bergie exclaimed. "It works! Let's see what she'll do." He turned the crank on the telephone several times and they tried it again. This time the spark jumped when the wires were a half inch apart.

"Wow! I wonder how far we can make the spark jump? Wind 'er up this time," Scooter urged.

Bergie began cranking vigorously. He was about to stop cranking when there was an explosion! The top shot off the jar, and broken glass flew in all directions. Smoke puffed out as if someone had exploded a firecracker inside the jar. The smell of burning rubber filled the room and burned their nostrils. The boys looked at each other in bewilderment.

"What the . . . ! What happened?" Bergie asked.

"Beats me." Scooter shook his head as he reached over to pick up a piece of the jar that had been blown to the floor. It was hot to the touch and he withdrew his hand quickly.

"Are you kids all right?" It was Scooter's grandfather calling from the bottom of the stairs.

"I think so," Scooter replied. "I think we caused an explosion, but I don't know why."

"Do I smell rubber burning?" the old man called.

"That's what it smells like to me, but there's no . . ." He paused as he looked at what was left of the jar. "I wonder if the static electricity ignited the rubber cement?" Scooter guessed.

By this time Grandfather Secory was at the door of Scooter's room. "Pugh!" he said. "You better open a window and air this room out. What happened?" When he heard the story, and looked at the jar, he agreed with Scooter's assessment. "I suggest you use shellac to affix that foil to the jar next time. I don't think it's flammable. But at least you know the concept works. You two ever think of going into the business of making bombs for the Allies?" And with that the old man left the boys to air out the bedroom and clean up the mess they made.

*****

The next day before practice, Scooter told Coach Coors about the ill-fated experiment.

"Hmm," was the physics teacher's first reaction as he furrowed his brow. "Rubber cement is certainly flammable enough, but for there to be an ignition the spark had to have come in contact with the rubber cement somehow. Your grandfather's idea of using shellac is a good one. Be sure you press all the bubbles out of the foil, at least as much as you can. And go easy with that old crank telephone. They were designed to send an electrical signal over long distances. They can generate quite a charge. I'm sure pleased you're not picking glass out of your hands, or worse. I don't need to lose both my starting centerman and guard to a physics experiment gone ka-blooie. Now, get ready for practice. We have an important game coming up."

When Scooter got to the locker room, the mood was up-beat. It was still vacation, and the guys were trading stories of the Christmas gifts they had received. The war production put a crimp in folks' ability to give gifts. The Sears and Roebuck catalog was some 200 pages smaller than in pre-war years, and many items pictured carried the label "Subject to Ration." Others had captions like a Sears wringer washing machine that said "Now on Active Duty." It indicated the item was being made only for war production and was not available to the general public.

Scooter was secretly sure his aviator model watch was far and away the finest gift anyone had received that year. But he wasn't showing it off on his wrist. Instead, he kept it in a box in the top drawer of his dresser, ready for the time when it would be "on active duty."

After practice, Scooter left for his delivery job at Cashmere's Grocery Store, and Woody, Bergie, Dutchie, and Doolie walked home together.

"Bergie, how do you pronounce airport in German—Flughafen?" Woody wanted to know.

"You still teaching yourself German?" Dutchie asked.

"A little here, a little there," was the answer.

"Airport is pronounced 'FLOOGHhahv'n," Bergie instructed.

"FLOOKhahv'n?"

"Floogh doesn't rhyme with Luke. You have to scrape your throat like you're scraping out a loogie. More like FLUEkkkk-hahv'n."

"FLOOGHhahv'n."

That's it. FLOOGHhahv'n. And FLOOGHplahn is flight plan."

"Thanks, Bergie. Nice to have a private tutor."

"So Woody, what's the Question of the Day?" Dutchie asked his smaller friend.

"Let's see. The Question of the Day. What day is it?"

"The worst day of the year. December 26," replied Dutchie.

"Why is that the worst day of the year, I wonder?" Woody wanted to know.

"Is that your question for today?"

"No, it's just a normal, pedestrian-type wonder. Why is this the worst day of the year?"

"Because we have to wait a whole year before it's

Christmas again. When I was little, I used to wake up on December 26 and be sad, because I realized it would be 364 days before Christmas came again," Dutchie said as they walked along. "You know what I wondered when I woke up this morning?"

"So you had a Question of the Day?" Woody observed. "What was it?"

"I wondered if I would see another Christmas."

"Yeah . . ."

"So I was hoping you had a happier Question of the Day to replace mine."

"You kinda need a better question, don't you. Well here's a better one. I wonder what cruel person decided to put an *s* in the word *lisp*."

Dutchie was squinting and staring straight ahead trying to understand Woody's lisp joke when he saw it. It was a black 1939 Chevrolet with a white star on the door—an army car. It came slowly down the street, as if the driver was looking for a house number. The boys stopped talking as the Chevrolet slowly passed them.

Dutchie let out a breath. "At least he didn't stop at my house. I wonder who he's looking for?"

They walked on in silence. The sight of the Chevrolet and the message its driver surely carried took all the funny out of "who put an *s* in the word *lisp*." They had walked about a half a block farther when the Chevrolet passed them again, this time in the direction they were walking. Good God, don't let him stop at my house, thought Dutchie as new fears for his brother Rich filled his head. But the car's brake lights came on several houses short of the Nagtzaam house. The car pulled over to the curb and stopped, and the officer got out and headed straight across the street to the Pitre residence.

From across the street the boys could see that the flag in the Pitres' front window had three stars. One of them was already gold, the other two were blue. The officer knocked on the door, and when Mrs. Pitre came out, she let out a gasp and put her hands to her mouth. The officer didn't have to say a word. She knew at once why he was on her front porch and what he would tell her.

"The War Department regrets to tell you . . ."

Mrs. Pitre began to sob uncontrollably and leaned heavily on the door jamb. The boys averted their eyes to respect the mother's shock and grief.

The boys were not the only ones to see the black Chevrolet with the star on the side go up and then down the street, nor were they the only ones to watch where it stopped, knowing what message it carried. It was like the ice cream wagon that came through the neighborhood in the summertime. Even if you didn't hear the tinkle of its bells, you knew when it was going by. In much the same way, the driver of the black Chevrolet didn't need to blow his horn to let people know he was there. They just knew. They were somehow compelled to look out their windows and see him there.

Mrs. McCabe, the next door neighbor, came out of her front door wringing her hands in her apron and disappeared into the front room of the Pitres' house. Dutchie's mother wasn't far behind, hurrying over to the Pitres to do what she could for the family. And throughout the neighborhood prayers were said—some for the grieving family who now had lost two sons to battle, others thanking God that the Chevrolet hadn't stopped in front of their own house.

The boys walked a bit farther and reached Dutchie's front walk. As they did, Woody broke the silence that had hung over them since the Chevrolet stopped. "I have another question," he said, almost to nobody in particular. When Dutchie didn't respond but just stood there waiting for him to finish, Woody looked up into his friend's eyes and asked simply, "Why?" and he turned to finish his walk home. Dutchie and Bergie were silent with the same question.

The grapevine in the small town was so efficient that the Pitres' tragedy was the topic of dinner conversation for many families in Grand Harbor that evening. When the *Tribune* came out the next day, it contained the news of Pfc. Donald Pitre killed on Leyte in the Philippines. An article beneath it related the death of Alvin Ross Gillett, also killed on Leyte. When the ladies of the town gathered to roll bandages in the armory the next day, they said a prayer for the Pitres and Gilletts as well as a silent prayer for themselves. For the most part the women worked in silence that day. Women don't wear war well.

In the Nelson household, the news of the death of Donald Pitre and Alvin Gillett was especially troubling. It meant that the war was not going well in the Philippines, and for there to be any news at all of Uncle Lou, the Americans needed to liberate that nation of islands—all 1,100 of them. So the waiting continued.

Chapter 13

I'm in the Air Corps, Mrs. Jones

"Wake up, sleepy-head. It's almost noon and there's a letter come for you."

Woody struggled to get the sleepers out of his eyes and the sleep webs out of his brain. He stretched and yawned and finally realized what his mother had said.

"A letter? Who from?" he asked.

"It's real official looking, and it's down on the dining room table . . ." by that time she was talking to the back of his pajamas. At the words *official looking* he had bolted out of bed and down the stairs.

The return address was the U.S. Army Air Corps. His heart sank. His rejection letter, no doubt. He opened it reluctantly and saw the seal of the United States of America was at the top.

24 December 1944

Mr. Woodrow Peabody Nelson
310 Howard Street
Grand Harbor, Michigan

Dear Mr. Nelson:

You are advised that because of your outstanding score on your preliminary testing, you are invited to appear at the U.S. Army Air Corps Recruiting Center in Detroit, Michigan, for additional testing and a physical exam.

This second series of tests is administered to those candidates for induction into the Air Corps who the Corps feels may fit the requirements of size, temperament, and intelligence to become pilots of the Air Corps' most advanced combat airplanes.

Please report on 29 December at 09:00 hours. You can expect testing to be completed by 16:30 hours. You are requested to phone the Center and ask for Lieutenant Jenkins to confirm your intention to accept this invitation no later than 15:00 hours, 27 December 1944. Detailed driving directions, timetable, and other pertinent information are enclosed, as well as government authorization to purchase the necessary gasoline for the trip.

This opportunity to serve your country in an important capacity should be considered an honor, and we urge you to accept this invitation. Your country needs you.

Very truly yours,
J. Michael Hopkins
Major, U.S. Army Air Corps

Woody was trembling. He re-read the address. There was no other Woodrow Peabody Nelson at 310 Howard Street or any other street in Grand Harbor, Michigan. They must mean him.

"THEY MUST MEAN ME!" he shouted at the top of his lungs. "THEY MEAN ME!" he shouted at his mother who was standing aghast at the dining room door. Woody waved the letter in the air and began goose-stepping around the dining room table landing on each foot so hard the dishes in the china cabinet rattled.

When he reached the doorway where his mother stood, bewildered, Woody grabbed her around the waist and waltzed her around the table with him. At the top of his lungs he sang, "I'm in the Air Corps, Mrs. Jones. I'm in the Air Corps, Mrs. Jones," to the tune of Irving Berlin's popular song "This Is the Army, Mr. Jones."

"Woodrow, stop it! Let me go! What's this all about? Woodrow, we're going to break my good china. Please, let me go. Tell me what the letter says. Woodrow Peabody! Let me go!" she exclaimed laughing and breathless by now after several trips around the table.

"That's what it says. 'Woodrow Peabody!' They mean me, a.k.a. Woody. They want me in the Air Corps. The test I thought I flunked? I passed. I mean I really passed! Oh boy, did I pass! I need to go to Detroit on Friday. I need to call them right now. How do you call

Detroit? Where is the number? Must be on the second sheet. Here it is. How do you call Detroit?"

Mrs. Nelson stood with her arms folded as she saw the unabashed joy gushing out of her son. He's just a boy, she thought, as he talked proudly to the Air Corps people in Detroit. For now she would do her best to share his joy and not spoil this moment for him. But she was also aware of what agony it would be to watch him leave to go into the service of his country, just as she watched her brother go some six years ago. It would add an even more chilling dimension to her waiting. She envisioned her heart as one big waiting room and wondered how much waiting it could take. She was reminded of the quote, "They also serve who only stand and wait." How true, she thought, how true.

*****

Woody's letter was the topic of conversation on the walk to basketball practice. "That's great, Woody. Really great." Bergie patted his small friend on the back.

"This means you'll miss the game Friday night," Scooter reminded him.

"Oh, geesh. That's right. How long does it take to get here from Detroit?"

"Several hours. But the game's not here, it's in Kalamazoo," Doolie reminded him.

"Geesh. Looks like a visit to the coach's office is in

order. I feel so bad for you guys."

"Whaddya mean, so bad for us?" Doolie wanted to know.

"Looks like I won't be around to bail your sorry butts out of trouble against Captain Hook."

"If we need bailing from the likes of you, we are sorry," Doolie said.

"Who's Captain Hook?" Bergie asked.

"His name is Lou Noble and he plays for Kalamazoo. He's six-foot-six and leads the league in scoring and in rebounding. They call him Captain Hook because he has a hook shot from anywhere and he seldom misses."

"How do you know so much about this guy, Woody?"

"My Uncle Jim lives in Kalamazoo and he brought over some newspaper clippings when we were together for Christmas. He knew I made the team and figured I'd need all the help I could get when we played Kalamazoo."

"Six-foot-six, huh? If we all took Bergie down and sat on him, suppose we could stretch him to six-foot-six?"

"You'd have to put another 50 pounds on him, as well. Captain Hook weighs 220."

"Cripes sakes," Dutchie exclaimed, "that's more than Bergie and Woody put together!"

"Do you want to know what I wonder?" Woody asked

reflectively.

"Is this the Question of the Day for December 27, 1944?" Dutchie asked.

"It sure is. I wonder how you guys are going to win without me," Woody replied and took off running before his friends could punish him for being so cocky. But he wasn't fast enough, and when they caught him they washed his face in the snow until he cried "Uncle."

*****

When they got to the gym, Woody went right to the coach's office to tell him of his conflict with the Air Corps testing and Friday's game.

"Come in, Woodrow. What's on your mind? How are you coming on your Leyden jar? Hmm?"

"Just fine, sir. Doolie, I mean, Lester and I are working on our second version. The first one worked real good, but we found some thinner foil and I think that will work even better," Woody responded.

"What are you using to glue the foil to the inside of your jar?"

"Liquid paraffin. It's hard to work with because it becomes a solid real quick, but I learned to work with a warm jar. That helps."

"Good, good. So what can I do for you, Woodrow?"

"I'm sorry I can't go with you to the game Friday night. I have a test . . ." Woody told the coach the whole story and finished up with, "If I get done early enough, I'll drive to Kalamazoo. I'd like to seen Captain Hook play."

"So you know about Mr. Noble, do you?"

"Yes, sir. Read about him in the Kalamazoo newspaper, and my Uncle Jim has seen him play."

"Have you given any thought as to how we could stop this Captain Hook?"

"Well, maybe we could keep him off the offensive backboard by having Bergie play up near the free throw line. That would draw him away from the basket so our forwards have a chance at the offensive rebounds, at least. Then if we could have Bergie not collapse to the basket when we're on the defensive and block Noble out—it could force him to go over Bergie's back. He might commit a foul or two."

"Mmmm. Well, thank you, Mr. Nelson, and I wish you well on your test on Friday. I'm sure you'll acquit yourself just fine."

"Thank you, sir," Woody said and left to get ready for the practice.

*****

Woody left for Detroit on Thursday afternoon. He took the family's 1939 Ford. The tires were bad, but his father had borrowed two extra spares that were stowed on the floor of the back seat. The two spares were in worse condition than those on the car, but tires were being rationed. No matter how much money you had, if you didn't have the right ration coupons, you got no tires. You simply had to patch and repair the ones you had.

Woody was well prepared for his journey. He had a box lunch of cold fried chicken, potato salad, and some homemade bread, and a map of Michigan, and another of the city of Detroit. His suitcase contained a change of clothes and his basketball gear. He had a reservation for a room at a YMCA which was not far from the recruiting center.

Getting lost was not what worried Woody. Grand River Drive, although it was called other things in different parts of Michigan, stretched from Grand Harbor—Highway 45—all the way to downtown Detroit. His real concerns were finding service stations that were open when he needed gas and getting back in time for the basketball game.

Since there wasn't much traffic on the highway, Woody made what he thought was good time. The Nelsons' car had no radio, and before it got dark the monotony of the drive was broken up by the red and white signs spaced about 30 yards apart that advertised a shaving cream. The first one he saw simply said "Ben." Then 30 yards later a sign said "Met Anna."

"Made a hit" was on the next sign, followed by "Neglected beard." "Ben-Anna split" and "*Burma-Shave*" were on the last two signs.

Nearing Lansing there was another set of signs:

They missed
The turn
Car was whizz'n
Fault was her'n
Funeral his'n
Burma-Shave

It got dark early and Woody couldn't read the Burma-Shave signs any longer, but every so often there was a small town to break up the monotony. Towns like Williamston, Webberville, Fowlerville, Howell, and Brighton were smaller than Grand Harbor, each with a traffic signal and a few stores. When he finally arrived at the outskirts of Detroit, Grand River Avenue broadened into a six-lane boulevard. The blocks and blocks of stores seemed endless. At last he spotted the tall buildings of the downtown area. Consulting his map, he found the YMCA without difficulty.

Woody parked the car in a lot across the street and got his suitcase and box lunch out of the back seat. He turned to look at the large building with the big red neon sign spelling out YMCA. For a time he fought panic. What was he doing here by himself? It was the first time he was alone and away from his home and parents. In the familiar environment of the family car, he felt connected to his family and his home. But standing in the streets of Detroit by himself was a different matter. He swallowed hard and walked across the street to the building's entrance. He hadn't come this far to chicken out.

An old man who had missed some of his whiskers when he shaved that morning was behind an oak counter inside. "If yer looking for a room, we're full up," he said, eyeing Woody's suitcase.

Great! Now what am I going to do? Woody thought. But deciding it was too soon to give up, he confronted the man. "I'm supposed to have a room set aside for me."

"You got a reservation? That's different. Name?"

"Nelson. Woodrow Nelson."

The man ran a forefinger yellowed by years of cigarette smoking down the lines of a ledger book.

"Yup. Ya' do. Room 512. Be two dollars and ten cents in advance. Ya' get a dime back if'n when ya' bring yer key back. Ya' need to sign here." He turned the book around and pointed to a line beside Woody's name.

"Ya' goin' in tomorrow?"

"I'm here to take some tests."

"Them's what's goin' in tomorrow 'll be up and making a heck of a racket 'bout six. Be hard to sleep through the noise they'll be making. Cafeteria's open at six, serves until 9:30."

"Thanks."

Woody took the key, and the old man came from behind the counter and shuffled toward the elevator. "Kid that's supposed to run this went in day b'fore yesterday. Think we can find someone to work? Everbody and his kid brother's off fighting in the gol'dang war. Lucky they can find old fogies like me ta keep the place runnin."

The old man clanged the wire door shut behind Woody and turned the handle on a wheel. The elevator groaned and started a slow ascent to the fifth floor, where the old man turned the wheel back and forth to get the floor of the elevator even with the fifth floor. After several unsuccessful tries, the old man stopped the elevator about three inches above the floor and yanked the door open. "Watch yer step. Down the hall to the right, sonny. Crappers at either end of the hall. Sleep tight."

The elevator clanged shut behind him and Woody found room 512 just a few doors down the dimly lit hall. He unlocked the door and felt for the light switch.

The cramped room had a bed, a very small desk with a wooden chair, a dry sink with a bowl and a pitcher of water, and smelled strongly of cigarette smoke. Woody put his suitcase down, set the box lunch on the desk, and tried out the bed. The springs sagged and the pillow was thin. He stretched out and folded his hands behind his head and stared at the ceiling. A blinking light down on the street cast a shadow, making parts of the ceiling go from red to gray, then back to red. It was only one night, he told himself. He could survive.

Woody yawned, suddenly realizing he was both very tired and very hungry. He got up and undid the string on the box lunch. Several napkins covered the food, and under them was a note in his mother's handwriting. "Do good, honey. We're so proud of you and will be thinking of you." The note was welcome, but also brought the loneliness back in full force.

His mother's fried chicken was the best, and Woody devoured it and the potato salad in a short time. Then he washed up and decided a good night's sleep before the tests would be a good thing. Although the bed squeaked at his every movement and the pillow was hardly worth its name, he fell asleep immediately.

*****

"Your name?" the young officer at the reception desk of the recruiting center asked. He had numerous battle ribbons on his shirt and his name plate read "Jenkins."

"Nelson, Woodrow Nelson."

"Can I see some identification, Mr. Nelson?"

"I have my letter—the invitation you sent me." Woody handed it to the young officer, who awkwardly reached to take it with his left hand. As Woody studied the officer more closely, he saw a right arm, but no right hand.

"That will do. All right, Mr. Nelson. Please have a seat in the room to your left. We'll be getting started soon."

There were six young men already in the room and five more joined them before another officer entered.

"Good morning, gentlemen. I'm Major Hopkins. Thank you all for coming. This morning you will be given a battery of physical exams, eye tests, and some coordination/reaction tests. That should be done at 11:00 hours. Then the real fun begins. There will be math tests, physics tests, and some psychological testing.

"An airplane is a marvelous marriage of math and physics with a little chemistry thrown in. We think a good pilot must understand the forces in play when a plane is in the air. Your comprehension of the elements that keep the plane in the air is important, but as you know, we're fighting a war and we don't have time to give you an education in the sciences. So your performance in these examinations will be the criteria the Air Corps will use to choose candidates for flight school.

"These tests," he continued, "are designed to test your knowledge, your ability to reason logically and concisely, and make quick and accurate decisions. And believe me, they do just that. Now, let's get started with the physicals. If you gentlemen will follow me please."

As they lined up to follow the major, Woody noticed they were all the same size. No Dutchies, no Bergies, no Scooters. They were all Woodys, and he made the connection like sparks leaping between the wires on his Leyden jar. Dutchie, Bergie, Doolie, and Scooter were all too big! There was a size requirement, and those big oafs were too big! They couldn't fit in the cockpit of a fighter plane. Suddenly being small was very big. Take that, Doolie, ya' big bully, he thought with a smile on his face.

Chapter 14

Lou from Kalamazoo

Woodrow Peabody Nelson finished the tests before anyone else. So much ahead of everyone else that the officer with one hand, Lieutenant Jenkins, asked him if he was quitting.

"No," Woody said. "I thought we were supposed to go as fast as we could. I'm finished."

The young lieutenant tried to look nonchalant and hide his disbelief, but Woody noticed. For a split second he wondered if he should take the test back and review his work. No, he decided. He had done his best.

"Very good, Mr. Nelson. Please report to Major Hopkins for your exit interview, then you're free to go. You'll be hearing from the corps one way or the other. Thank you for coming."

Woody felt like he should salute or something, but he just left and found the major's office. He knocked on the wavy glass in the door. The major looked surprised to see him.

"Yes?"

"Lieutenant Jenkins said I needed to see you for an exit interview."

"Oh, yes. Come in and sit down. I wasn't expecting anyone this early. So you've finished, have you?"

"Yes, sir," Woody replied, taking the chair the major had indicated.

"You are . . .?"

"Nelson, Woodrow Nelson."

"Yes, Nelson. I have your file here. There are just some questions we need to have answered. Let's see. Here we are. Mr. Nelson, are you susceptible to car motion sickness?"

"No, sir."

"Trouble with your sinuses?"

"No, sir."

"Have you ever been diagnosed with inner ear disorders?"

"No, sir."

"Do you have fluency in a second language?"

"I speak some German."

The major looked up from his paper. Woody couldn't tell if he was surprised or suspicious.

"How is it that you speak some German?"

"I've taught myself, sir. In case I got shot down, I could make my way."

"*Verstehen Sie Luftwaffe?*"

"*Ya, Ich verstehe Luftwaffe. Mann sagt auf Englisch* German Army Air Corps. *Nicht wahr?*"

"*Ya.*" The major regarded him thoughtfully. "Does anyone else in your family, parents or grandparents, speak German?"

Oops. For a moment Woody was worried he had gone too far with the German thing. "No, sir. My family are all Swedes. I have a Jewish friend whose family fled Germany in 1936. He's helped me with the pronunciation some, but mostly I learned by myself."

"In case you got shot down, you could make your way, is that right?"

"Yes sir."

*****

When the major dismissed him, Woody walked the three blocks to the lot where he had parked the car. There was a basketball game to get to. He stopped to get gas at a nearby filling station, and when the attendant came out to pump the gas and check the oil, Woody asked him how to get to US 12. The directions were easy and in no time Woody was headed toward Kalamazoo.

Again it was the Burma-Shave signs that broke up the monotony of the snowy rural landscape. One read:

Let's make Hitler
And Hirohito
Look as sick as
Old Benito

Lou from Kalamazoo

Buy defense bonds

Burma-Shave

When the early darkness set in and Woody was no longer able to read the Burma-Shave signs, he stopped at a roadside diner in Jackson and ordered a hamburger and a shake to go. The restaurant didn't have any paper cups, so he had to drink the shake while the hamburger was frying.

"Don't you know there's a war on, sonny?" the waitress snarled at him as she explained the lack of paper cups.

"Really? I hadn't heard. Whose winning?" Woody wanted to say, but decided against it.

Woody got back on the road and was just thinking he might get to Kalamazoo in time for warm-ups when he felt the car begin to shake. The steering wheel began to vibrate in his hands—a little at first, then almost violently. No! A flat tire. He guided the car onto the shoulder at an intersection of a country road and when it stopped, he got out to find his worse fears realized. If he didn't change the tire quickly, he'd miss the game.

Fortunately there was a partial moon, and although it was on the left side of the car, the light reflecting off the snowy landscape helped him see what he was doing. He opened the trunk and took out the jack and the spare tire. When the tire hit the ground, it didn't bounce. It was as flat as the one on the right front side of the car. He silently thanked his father for his foresight to send him off with two other spares. He opened the back door and pulled out one of the spares, but to his dismay it didn't bounce either. Just his luck the third spare would also be flat, he imagined. He returned the second spare and went around to see the condition of the third. It was firm! Yes, it bounced like a ball.

It took Woody a precious 30 minutes to change the tire. Before he was finished his hands were nearly frozen and his knuckles were bruised, but he was back on the road. He held one hand in front of the heater blower, then the other, all the while praying that he wouldn't have another flat—the consequences of which he didn't want to even think about.

When he finally arrived at Kalamazoo High School, the scoreboard read Home 21, Visitors 15, with six minutes to go in the first half. The ball was passed to Captain Hook, who gave Bergie a head fake to the left but pivoted right, holding the ball with his arm extended and then arching a hook shot over Bergie. The ball went through the basket touching only the net, swish. The Pirates took the ball out of bounds and worked the ball to Doolie, who went in for a lay-up. But Doolie was fouled and missed the shot. He made one of his two underhand free shots: Home 23, Visitors 16.

When Kalamazoo brought the ball down the court, it became clear what their game plan was. Get the ball to Captain Hook. He would head fake one way and deliberately extend his arm straight out from his body and arch his trademark hook shot toward the basket. There would be another swish and another two points. It seemed there was nothing Bergie could do against him. The score was 28-21 when the buzzer signaled the end of the half.

Woody had no idea where the visitor's locker room was and so he waited to follow the team. They ran right to the corner of the gym where he was standing. Bub Denton was the first to spot him.

"Hey, it's Woody! You made it from Detroit? Come on, let's get you dressed."

Woody waited with his suitcase, patting each player on the back as he went by, intending to follow the last one. But the last player was followed by Coach Coors, who stopped when he saw Woody.

"Woodrow, looks like your Captain Hook is everything you said he was."

"Yes, sir. I only saw about the last six minutes, but does he always head fake one way and pivot the other?"

"Hmm." The coach furrowed his brow and stroked his chin as they walked. "Yes, I believe he does. Why?

What did you see?"

They were now outside the locker room door. "Well, he extends his arm with the ball so far out that the arc he creates makes it impossible for anyone to defend against it. But if he always telegraphs the way he's going to pivot, he's looking the wrong way for a second. Maybe we should have the guard who plays away from the direction of Hook's head fake go after the ball when he extends his arm like he does. It's just sitting out there for a second, just waiting to be stolen."

"That might work. Nothing else we've tried does. You better get dressed," the coach said as they entered the locker room.

*****

"Okay, men. It's almost time to go back out there. Woodrow noticed something that may help us against big Lou Noble, or Captain Hook as Woody calls him." There were some chuckles around the room. Woody noticed he had become "Woody."

"I want the guards to watch him when the ball comes to him. If he head fakes away from you, I want you to start towards him, and when he sticks out that big paw of his with the ball extended away from his body, I want you to go for it. Try to swipe the ball out of his outstretched hand. The other guard has to watch for the ball to come his way. Maybe we can steal it and get a fast break or two going.

"Woody, you start at guard with Mr. Denton, and we'll see if we can steal a ball or two from Captain Hook, or at least take him off his stride. If we can't stop him, it's gonna' be a long ride home!"

Captain Hook controlled the tip-off to start the second half, and Kalamazoo worked the ball into their end of the court. When the pass came to Captain Hook, he gave Bergie a head fake. At the same time, Woody broke for the spot where he was sure Hook would extend the ball. Sure enough he did, and Woody batted it out of his outstretched hand. Bub cut in front of the man he was guarding, picked up the ball, and raced down the court for an easy lay-up. Kalamazoo 28, Grand Harbor 23.

When Kalamazoo came down the floor, they again worked the ball around until they could get it to Captain Hook. This time he head faked toward Woody. Satisfied Woody was no threat, he extended his arm to pivot the other way only to have Bub there to swat the ball out of his extended hand. There was no chance for a fast break and an easy lay-up, but the Pirates took the ball down the court and worked it in to Dutchie for an easy lay-up; 28-25.

When Kalamazoo took the ball out of bounds, they again worked it in to Captain Hook. But aware that Woody and Bub were on to him, the Kalamazoo star changed his style and omitted his head fake. Uncomfortable without his old routine, however, he missed the shot, and because Bergie had boxed the big guy out, Jacob Merrill came down with an easy rebound.

When the Pirates set up for their next shot, Captain Hook fouled Bergie. Bergie made only one of his two shots, making the score 28-26, and Kalamazoo's coach asked for a time out.

*****

As Coach Coors had predicted, it would be a long ride home if they lost. Although they had succeeded in distracting Captain Hook and held him to only 9 points in the second half after he scored 20 in the first, the Pirates went for about eight minutes without making a basket. In addition, Bergie had fouled out guarding the Hook, and the Pirates wound up losing by two points, 42-40.

Scooter and Bergie had offered to ride home with Woody to keep him company. Scooter wanted to know all about the Air Corps tests, and they rehashed the game as well. "If you had noticed what Captain Hook was doing at the beginning of the game, we'd a killed 'em," was Scooter's assessment.

"I was lucky to get there at all," Woody answered. "I had a flat tire on the way from Detroit. About froze my hands off and look at my knuckles. I think that white stuff you can see is bone. And after I pulled two spares out of the car that were flats, I thought I might have to spend the night in some farmer's barn."

"I can tell you Coors was hoping you'd get there. Bub told me he asked the guys on the bench several times if anyone had seen you," said Scooter.

"If only I hadn't fouled out," Bergie lamented. "Captain Hook made seven points on free throws."

"How many points did Mr. Lou Noble have altogether?" Woody asked.

"He made 29," Scooter said.

They rode on in silence watching the snowflakes rush past the windshield. Scooter was soon nodding his head. Bergie was staring out the side window.

Woody was unsettled. They hadn't won, but everyone on the team knew it was his advice to Coach Coors that had given them the chance to win. Coors had acknowledged as much in front of the team. He had even referred to him as "Woody." Then he had driven over 400 miles on his first trip away from home alone. He had changed his first flat tire. But back in Detroit, Michigan, there were two officers grading papers who were skeptical that he had finished so fast. He wondered how he had done. It was the Question of the Day, if anyone asked.

The headlights of the Ford continued to pierce the

onslaught of snowflakes as Woody went through the math problems in his mind again, at least the ones he could remember. He thought he had them all right. The physics test was harder. There were one or maybe two questions he was unsure of, but he was confident of the rest.

The psychological testing was similar to the test Woody had taken back when the recruiter came to the high school. The questions tried to determine if you were brave, if you could make decisions, and if you could follow orders. Woody had answered the questions the way he thought the Air Corps wanted them to be answered. Now he worried what the people who graded the tests would think if they figured out by his answers that he had figured out the test. He recalled how Major Hopkins had looked surprised—or was it suspicious?—when Woody told him he spoke some German. Did the major think it was good he taught himself, or did he suspect he was looking at a 17-year-old spy?

There was one thing Woody was certain of. He was desperate to be a fighter pilot. That would show everyone once and for all that he was as good as any of them, and better than most. What he didn't know was that it was something he needed to show himself as well.

*****

The Nelsons were waiting up for their son. Woody

could see the relief in his mother's eyes when she met him at the back door. His father's concern was more practical. He was pleased to see the car in one piece but noticed the right front tire had been changed. The three sat around the dining room table as Woody recounted the events of the trip over hot chocolate and a plate of cookies. They talked until his father signaled it was time for bed. He had to work in the morning. Saturday or not, the army needed the tank parts his factory made.

Woody stayed up to read the newspapers of the past two days and unwind over another cup of hot chocolate. Thursday's paper reported a large convoy of American ships in the Philippines. The report was out of Japan and said that the Americans were poised for a large-scale invasion of the Philippine mainland. There was another article telling of the death of a Private Loren Dexter, killed on Leyte.

Friday's paper reported that American bombers relentlessly pursued surviving Japanese warships and had sunk three destroyers and a battleship. In Europe, the south flank of the Nazi lines was yielding to Patton's Third Army. But it also reported that the total killed in Britain by the V-1 buzz bombs had reached 8,098 with 21,137 seriously injured. Woody wondered what the casualties would have been if those V-1s were reliable and accurate.

Woody paused over a story that said U.S. casualties had reached 612,441 killed, wounded, or missing in action, not even counting the casualties of the Battle of the Bulge. It occurred to him that he had met one of those casualties this morning—Lieutenant Jenkins, who would forever be without a right hand. He hoped he would meet another soon—his Uncle Lou. That would be the other Lou from Kalamazoo. The one that called his mother "Sweetcakes."

Chapter 15

A Shocking Experience

The first day back to school was the deadline for the Leyden jar assignment competition, and the seventh hour physics class was buzzing. There were big jars and small, some crude and some that displayed thoughtful craftsmanship. One jar used water inside instead of using foil.

"Now remember," Mr. Coors was saying, "our criteria for the winning entry will be the jar's capacity as measured by the length of the spark that will be generated. What I'm going to do is connect each jar in turn to this electric Wimshurst machine. After a one-minute charge, we'll bring its negative pole—that is, the wire attached to the outside of the jar—slowly up to the positively charged wire until the spark jumps the gap. We'll measure the gap, and, of course, the longest gaps will show us the best constructed jars.

"In this way we'll determine the three finalists and then perform another test to measure the capacity of each finalist's jar."

While all the jars worked, the gaps on Scooter and Bergie's, Woody and Doolie's, and Marv Peters and Jake

Merrill's jars were longest, each measuring over an inch. Mr. Coors began the final tests with Woody and Doolie's jar. He hooked the wire coming out of the top of the jar to a voltage meter and repeated the experiment. This time he let the Wimshurst run to charge the jar as he spoke.

"The Leyden jar was just a curiosity for a long time. It was called a condenser because scientists thought of electricity as a matter that could be condensed." The Wimshurst machine hummed as the teacher continued talking. "Nowadays, it's called a capacitor and is being used in all sorts of electrical devices. Experiments are also being conducted to see if a capacitor can be made out of smaller, solid materials." The Wimshurst was continuing to hum. Woody was becoming concerned. The jar was building up a considerable amount of electricity. But Mr. Coors didn't seem concerned and continued lecturing.

"I have a sample of such a material," he said as he reached for a piece of hard brown material and began to bring it over Woody's jar.

ZAP!!!

A huge spark leaped out of the top of the jar along the wire, and Mr. Coors's hand received the entire discharge. The shock threw him against the blackboard where his head hit with a sickening thud. He slid down the wall to the floor.

The class was momentarily stunned. Then Woody leaped from his seat and raced around the presentation table. His teacher's eyes were crossed and he had a blank look on his face. Woody was afraid the worst had happened. His Leyden jar had killed the teacher! Doolie, who had followed Woody to the front of the room, bent over the teacher and reported, "He's breathing!"

"Somebody get the principal, quick!" Woody yelled as he unplugged the humming Wimshurst machine.

Woody and Doolie tried to coax the teacher into consciousness. Finally, Mr. Coors's eyes uncrossed and he picked up his head. "Whad hap—pen?"

"We're sure sorry, sir," Woody offered. "We should have warned you the jar was getting too charged up."

Struggling to get to his feet, Coors began rubbing the back of his head. "Whew!" he said finally. "I don't know whether to say that was the most electrifying experience I've ever had or the most shocking experience of my life. In any case, I'm stunned."

The concerned class laughed weakly.

"Mr. Coors! Mr. Coors! Are you all right? What happened?" demanded the principal as he came into the classroom, followed by a worried office secretary.

"I think I'll be all right. I just took about . . . oh, let me see . . . about 40,000 volts through my system. Volts don't kill you, but they sure can tickle your toes," he said, still rubbing the back of his head and smoothing out his hair. He looked at Woody and Doolie, who had slinked back to their seats. "And I suppose you two want extra credit for the performance of your jar, do you?"

The class laughed nervously.

"Well, we've probably had enough physics lessons for the day," Mr. Babcock announced and went to clear the guilty Leyden jar out of the way.

"DON'T," Woody started. But before he could get "TOUCH THAT" out, the principal's hand neared the recharged jar.

ZAP!!!

"OUCH!" The principal recoiled from the shock and his wire rim glasses went akimbo. Both the class and the teacher didn't know whether to laugh or not as the principal rubbed his hand.

"Fools rush in," he mumbled and then added more clearly, "I think I'll get back to the safety of the principal's office." Still rubbing his hand he hurried out of the room, his secretary following. When the door closed behind them, there was first a snicker, then a hearty laugh.

Doolie raised his hand. "Are you personally going to test all of the finalists' jars that way?" The class laughed freely again and the tension of the two incidents was broken. But Woody was still in a spin. For a moment he had really believed he had killed that good man—after he had let him be on the basketball team and all.

*****

At dinner that evening, Woody told his mother and father about Coach Coors getting the jolt from the Leyden jar and the principal's misadventure with the same jar a few moments later.

"Goodness gracious, I hope they don't hold you responsible for that." Woody still appreciated his mother's protectiveness.

"No. He did make us stay after school, though. We had to figure out the actual voltage he absorbed . . . about 46,000 volts."

"I'm surprised it didn't kill him," she exclaimed.

"Volts don't kill, my dear," Mr. Nelson replied. "Amps kill. Static electricity, while it may give you a considerable shock, carries no amperes and therefore, other than the shock value, is not dangerous."

"Well, I'm just glad he didn't get hurt and Woodrow isn't blamed."

"Stranger things have happened," his father agreed.

"Speaking of strange things," she changed topics. "Do you remember me telling you about the Boven lady who had a trance or a dream and saw her son getting injured in Belgium?"

"Was it Belgium? As I recall, she just knew it was in Europe."

"Maybe it was Europe, but now we know it was Belgium. She was at the armory rolling bandages again today and told us the rest of the story. He got home on furlough Sunday and he's still got some healing to do—still has his arm in a sling and walks with a cane and such. Anyway, he wanted to tell his family what happened to him, and Mrs. Boven stopped him and said, 'No. Let me tell you what happened.' Then she proceeded to tell him of what she saw in her dream or trance or whatever it was.

"When she finished, he confirmed the story right down to the description of the field, the road, and the white dog setting off the land mine. It even happened on the very day and at the very time she was in this trance—1:10 in the afternoon in Belgium, 7:10 in the morning here on November 11. He said that her story cleared up a mystery for him. The medics at the medical station where he was brought in later told him they couldn't figure out how he got there. It seems there was an empty cot and all of a sudden, Private Boven was lying in it, all bloody and broken. There was no record of anyone bringing him in, no one saw him being brought in, and he certainly couldn't have come in by himself. He was just there."

Woody stopped eating his mashed potatoes. "The monk . . . the one with no face and no feet? He brought him there?"

"What other explanation is there?"

Woody and his father looked serious.

"That's an interesting story," Mr. Nelson said after a moment's reflection. "And I can see you're inclined to believe her, Sarah, and so am I. I've often thought there's more to the universe than what can be seen and measured."

"I wonder," Woody said thoughtfully. "I wonder if this is a case of envisioning. You know, like I talked about before. If you can envision something, can you make it happen? Did it really happen and that enabled her to see it and him to get to the medics, or did she envision it and cause it to happen?"

There was a moment with only the sounds of eating and drinking. Then Woody said what was really on his mind. "I'd like to believe her. It's easy to believe that there was a monk who picked him up and carried him to the med station. And I'd like to believe that this monk was God or a guardian angel. But if the monk was God or a guardian angel, why didn't he disarm the mine before the dog stepped on it, or stand over it so no one stepped on it? Isn't that what God or a guardian angel would do?"

A Shocking Experience

*****

Laughter dispersed the cloud that usually hung over the Greenberg's dinner table as Bergie recounted the hilarious events that occurred in his physics class that afternoon. But the chuckles that came when Bergie described the principal's involvement were cut off by the intrusive ringing of the telephone. Since it was unusual for the phone to ring during the dinner hour, all eyes followed Nettie Abrams as she got up to answer it.

"Hello? Yes, it is. Yes, I am," was followed by silence as the aunt listened. "I'll be here," she said and then put the receiver back into its cradle and turned to address the group. By the look on her face, Bergie had already decided what the phone call was about. The United States government had figured out that his grandfather was making the timing devices for the German V-1 rockets that were terrorizing England.

"It was an officer of the Army Office of Strategic Services. He's coming over to talk about our father," she said very calmly. Samuel's mother gasped and the color drained out of his father's face. It only took a second for Isaac Greenberg to react. He stood up so violently that he knocked his chair over backward.

"*Schnell*, quickly Samuel," he hissed as if he were afraid someone was listening. "Go to your friend's house across the street and wait there until I come for you.

Herr Secory can be trusted. Go! *Mach schnell*! Say nothing to them about what's happening."

Samuel heard his father's last words as he was bolting through the front door.

He didn't hear his aunt's firm words to her brother. "Isaac. Sit down and gather your wits. The officer isn't coming to arrest you. This is America. The Gestapo doesn't run things here."

"What do you know of the Gestapo, sister? Were you there when they came to our house on Frederickstrasse? No! You were in the safety and comfort of your home here in America. Well, we were there and I will not allow my family to be subjected to that humiliation again! Ever!"

"Isaac. Now *you* are in the safety and comfort of my home in America. When the Gestapo came, did they give you the courtesy of a phone call? Did they ask if it was convenient to come at such and such a time?" Her voice was calm but firm. "I think not. This officer tracked me down, not you. He didn't indicate he knows you're here. Now calm yourself. We'll clear the dishes and put on a fresh pot of coffee for him. The man bears news of our father and I intend to hear him out—in the safety and comfort of my home!"

*****

Bergie held his finger on the bell at the Secorys'

home so its chimes kept ringing. Merrill Secory answered the door.

"Samuel, come on in. What's so urgent? You look as if you've seen a ghost."

Samuel brushed passed him into the room, where he met Scooter coming out of the kitchen. The rest of the Secory family followed bewildered by the commotion.

"Scoot! It's the army! They called. They know about my grandfather. They're coming for us. I need to hide until my father can come for me."

"The army's coming? What do they know about your grandfather? What's this all about, Samuel?" the old man asked. "I think you better sit down and tell me what's going on."

When Bergie had finished his story, the old man tried to reassure him. "Samuel, I doubt that your grandfather, a Jewish watch repairman, would have a trusted position in Germany's war production. But if he did, and the army found out about it and were going to arrest your family, they wouldn't announce it with a telephone call. Of course, you're welcome to stay here until things become clear."

*****

Until the black Chevrolet with the white star on its doors stopped in front of their modest house, the children of Ibrem Grünberg sat in agonizing silence. Although it was evening, there was enough moonlight to announce the car's presence in the neighborhood. Everyone in the Secory house stood in front of the windows. The car's lone occupant was a tall man in a long coat and an officer's cap who seemed to be carrying a small rectangular object.

"Unless these old eyes deceive me, if he's here to arrest your family, he's only armed with a picture frame," Merrill Secory observed.

*****

When Nettie Abrams took the officer's coat, it was clear he was unarmed, a fact that didn't seem to ease her brother's all-consuming fear.

"This is my brother, Isaac Greenberg, and his wife. May I give you some coffee?"

"No, thanks. I won't be long. I'm Captain Taylor," the officer said as he reached to shake Isaac's trembling hand, which came forth reluctantly. "You must be a son of Ibrem Grünberg. It would seem I've killed two birds with one stone." At that comment, Isaac Greenberg turned white and had to fight to keep himself from fainting from fear.

"I have quite a story to tell you about your father. I don't know how much you know of his activities, but I served for two years in the Netherlands and had connections with the Dutch underground. One of my contacts was a man named Henk Boersma, a dealer of watch parts. He supplied watch parts to your father over the years and in the past few years to a top-secret German company in Berlin—Askania. Your father was employed there against his will, manufacturing the timing devices for the V-1 rocket, what we call the buzz bomb.

"Through Henk Boersma, we learned that your father had figured out a way to sabotage the devices so they would fly over or fall short of their targets. Unfortunately, he couldn't ruin all of them or the Germans would become suspicious. But for months, the Germans couldn't figure out why their rockets were so unreliable. Out of 8,000, only 2,400 actually hit their mark. But those 2,400 caused 6,000 deaths and nearly 18,000 people seriously wounded.

"For a long time the German scientists thought it was the unstable nature of the fuel or the changes in barometric pressure that made the bombs unreliable. But it was Ibrem Grünberg. Because of your father's courageous work, it is estimated that as many as 14,000 lives were saved. Many, many more were saved from injury.

"These timing devices were powered by a small propeller which spun as the rocket traveled. Your father secretly built certain teeth in the watch-like gears that after so many revolutions would engage other gears and cause the device to fail. Thus, the rocket would become a dud or overshoot or undershoot its mark. It was done so cleverly that testing didn't reveal the flaw.

"Recently we learned that a young German rocket scientist named Werner von Braun tracked the errors to the timing devices and eventually to your father. I'm sorry to report that Frau Grünberg was arrested and brought to the weapons factory, where she was hanged in front of her husband's eyes. Then he was hanged, and their bodies were left hanging as a lesson to the rest of the workers in the factory."

The officer paused to let the meaning of his words sink in.

"For his efforts, Ibrem Grünberg has been posthumously awarded an honorary appointment as a member of the Order of the British Empire by the British and a citation 'from a grateful nation' signed by Winston Churchill, which I am honored to deliver to you. It is the highest honor the British government can give to a foreign national not in the armed services. It's the civilian equivalent to a Medal of Honor."

Isaac Greenberg needed to wipe the tears from his cheeks and catch his breath before he could speak. His words came out in a stammer.

"I thought you were coming to arrest me and my family."

The big army officer smiled. "This is America. I'd like to think that kind of behavior is what we're fighting against."

"By any chance, do you have word of the Goldfarb family of Frankfort?" Samuel's mother asked. She was desperate for news of her parents.

"Our best information is that Jewish families that were resettled were shipped to Eastern Germany or Poland. The unconfirmed reports we do have are not good. Strong men are saved for work in war material factories; woman and children are . . . not." The captain lowered his eyes and shook his head.

Samuel's mother began to cry softly.

Aunt Nettie understood what her father was trying to say when he wrote, "It's not so bad to lose your teeth if the food is rotten."

Chapter 16

The District Finals

On the Friday after Woody thought he killed his physics teacher, there was a letter waiting for him when he got home from school. It was from the Army Air Corps. He held it in his trembling hands for a moment before opening it. What if he didn't pass the test? What if he hadn't passed the physical? What if they suspected he was a German spy?

"Aren't you going to open it?" his mother finally asked.

He tore the envelope and took out the letter.

3 January 1945

Mr. Woodrow Peabody Nelson
310 Howard Street
Grand Harbor, Michigan

Dear Mr. Nelson:

You are advised that because of your outstanding score on your testing conducted on 29 December, you have been accepted as a candidate for induction into the U.S. Army Air Corps and to be assigned for flight training.

Please contact this office by phone if you intend to accept this invitation to serve in a very vital branch of your country's armed services. It is noted that you are still in high school, and the Corps encourages you to complete your secondary education. You may be inducted any time after you reach the age of 18, if you choose to do so.

Please inform this office of your intentions at your earliest possible convenience.

This opportunity to serve your country in an important capacity should be considered an honor. Many are tested, few are chosen, and we urge you to accept this invitation. Your country needs you.

Very truly yours,

Michael Hopkins
Major, U.S. Army Air Corps

Woody was shocked. He hadn't allowed himself to believe this was possible. Then suddenly the letter and its meaning swept over him like a wave. Being small and smart had its advantages. Wait till his buddies heard about this . . . That's Airman Nelson to you, civilian!

"Are you in the Air Corps, Mr. Jones?" his mother

asked, although she could tell by the look on his face. She hoped he couldn't see that her smile was forced.

*****

The basketball season played itself out. The rest of the schedule was relatively easy and the Pirates won by relying on the tried and true set plays, well executed, giving them the high percentage shots. Woody and Bub Denton played only at the end of the first half and the end of the game, either to give the other guards a rest or if Scooter or Marv Peters got into foul trouble (which never seemed to happen). Bub often wished he had more playing time, but Woody was just happy to be on the team. Sure, he wished he were tall, could make more baskets, and had great dribbling skills. But lately Woody had discoverd some things that were pretty neat—like that all the guys at the Air Corps test were short like he was, that he could do the Air Corps math problems in his head, that his Leyden jar had ended up winning the physics competition, that he had figured a way to stop Captain Hook when even the coach hadn't seen it. Woody began to see the world through different lenses, and it almost shocked him.

*****

The news of the war in the Pacific indicated the tide was beginning to turn toward the Allies. The headlines of the *Tribune* on January 8 announced the beginning of the invasion of Luzon, the main island of the Philippines. By January 22, the Americans were halfway to Manila, the Philippine capital. The troops' advance, however, came at the price of hundreds of lives lost.

One day it was reported that Sgt. La Penna, formerly listed as missing in action, was alive and safe in a German prisoner of war camp. The next day Willard Hyde, a paratrooper from Grand Harbor, was reported killed, apparently in the Battle of the Bulge. The same newspaper carried the story of Sgt. John Rosema, a tail gunner on a bomber that had been shot down. His family had been clinging to the hope that he had bailed out and might be a prisoner. Then on January 13 he walked into the family home unannounced and said, "Hello, folks!" It was the first time they had heard from or about him since the previous July. He was reported to be very thin and nervous but otherwise okay.

Those who read the newspaper stories could by now easily imagine the renewed hope in one household, grief in another, joy in another. The stories of war along with mind-numbing worry had become part of everyone's life.

*****

January 19, 1945
Somewhere in the ETO

To my darling wife:

It's been 675 days since my induction, 497 and a half days since I've seen you. That's way too long. Can you tell I've been counting?

My darling, I know I'm going to heaven when I die because I've had my Hell on earth. Hell is a forest in **CENSORED**. *And I've been there (unfortunately) and lived (fortunately) to forget about it (hopefully). Funny thing about war. At its rawest brutality and horror, you have to laugh about it and make jokes to survive it. You cannot attach any significance to its reality, or you lose touch with your own reality. And you must understand its insanity to remain sane.*

Yesterday, we snuck to the top of a hill where we spotted a convoy of Germans about a half a mile long coming through the valley. We were telephoning their position for an artillery barrage when the CO saw they were herding about 30 captured GIs along with them. Some of the GIs were not in good shape, stumbling along, and were holding up the convoy. We told the artillery boys not to fire, there were GIs down there. Suddenly the convoy came to a halt, they lined up the GIs and mowed them down with machine guns. The CO telephoned back with instructions to throw everything they had at 'em. Within seconds, a half a mile of Germans went up in smoke. If they hadn't murdered our boys, they might be alive today.

To see violent death on a daily basis and know the next death could be yours changes a person. I am not the same person who left you 497 days ago. My only hope is that I'm doing this so that our children will not have to experience this horror, and this keeps me going. In war, everyone is a casualty.

Now that we're in **CENSORED**, *we have to go from house to house 'cuz the Kraut soldiers are going into houses and stealing clothes to disguise themselves as citizens. Some of them are even trying to wear GI uniforms to fool us. But none of them know who won the World Series in 1939 or how to pronounce Arkansas or the words to "Mairzy Doats." Tragedy is, a lot of the soldiers we're capturing are 14- and 15-year-old kids.*

The slogan here is "Get home alive in '45." Oh, how I pray it will be so.

I miss you so very much, more than I know how to say on paper. I think of you all every day. God bless you and keep me until we meet again—"alive in '45." I love you very much and can't wait to be in your arms again.

Rich

"Where do you think he is, Gramps?" Scooter asked the old man, who was standing over the map of Germany with his yardstick and string.

"When he wrote that letter he was in a German town on the Moselle River named Trier."

"According to the papers, the Third Army is much farther than that now. And the Russians are only 165 miles from Berlin. At the rate things are going, there's not going to be much war left to fight by the time graduation comes around."

"I wouldn't be too sure about that. There's the mainland of Japan to conquer, and that may be the bloodiest battle of them all."

*****

On the same day, Woody heard the dull thud against the front door announcing that Doolie had delivered the *Tribune*. He retrieved it and spread it out on the floor. A headline on the front page caught his eye:

Commando Raid Frees 516 at Jap POW Camp

Survivors of Corregidor and Bataan Saved

Luzon - Men of Bataan, Corregidor and Singapore were snatched from under the flaming muzzles of Japanese guns last night in an exploit of unmatched daring. Some 400 men of the Sixth Ranger Battalion and Filipino guerrillas made a commando raid 25 miles behind Japanese lines to empty a prison camp and partially fulfill one of the objectives closest to Gen. Douglas MacArthur's heart. All but two of the men were brought out alive by the 121 Rangers, who stormed the prison stockade under the command of Lt. Col. Henry Mucci of Bridgeport, Conn.

Woody raced to the kitchen."Mom! Mom! They're starting to free some of the troops who were on Corregidor. Mom! Where are you?"

"Down the basement in the fruit cellar, honey," came her muffled voice.

Woody went to the basement steps and shouted down, "They've freed some POWs from Corregidor. That means some guys are getting out of Bataan alive."

At the sound of "Corregidor" Sarah Nelson forgot why she had gone to the fruit cellar and was now at the bottom of the basement steps. "Does it say who or how many?" she asked hopefully.

"They rescued 516, but it doesn't say who or anything."

"Oh God," she murmured, "let one of them be Lou."

Woody knew, of course, that nearly 15,000 families all over America were reading their papers and saying the same prayer. He knew God couldn't answer all those prayers with good news, but all his mother needed was just one of them to be answered—hers.

*****

The Pirates ended the regular season with only one

loss, the one against Kalamazoo and Captain Hook. That qualified them to play in the tournament for the state championship. The first game was played at Burton Gym in Grand Rapids against Godwin Heights Wolverines. In this case Wolverines were no match for Pirates. Bergie played like he was possessed—freed from the fear over his family—and had his best game of the season. His 18 points led the Pirates to an easy 48-17 victory, and visions of another state championship began to dance in the heads of the Pirates and their fans.

The next team they had to face was the Eagles of Grand Rapids Christian on the following Friday night. On Monday before practice, Coach Coors called Woody into his office.

"Woody, we play Christian High next. Your suggestions as to how to play them won the day for us last time. Do you have any different thoughts now?"

"That's the team with the Worst twins, right? Shoulda' named them the Best twins. I remember them. Let's see," Woody furrowed his brow. "I wish we could see them again. Maybe if we could watch them, something would come to us."

Coach Coors thought for a moment. "That's a good idea. They're playing tomorrow night. Would you be willing to take a ride and see a basketball game?"

"Sure would, but I think we should take Dutchie and

Bergie along. Maybe Scooter."

"And why should they come along?" asked the coach.

"Envisioning."

"Envisioning? And what, may I ask, is envisioning?"

"I've been thinking about it for a while. It's when you envision a certain action and that helps you carry out the action. If Bergie can watch Christian play, he can envision what he has to do to play well against them.

"And you call that envisioning?"

Suddenly, Woody realized that the whole idea probably sounded silly to the coach.

"Well, the more minds working on a problem, the better chance we'll find a solution," the coach agreed.

The decision to include Scooter was a good one, especially since the only person they could find with enough gas rations to get to Grand Rapids and back was Scooter's grandfather, Merrill Secory. His 1937 Packard was big enough to carry all six of them.

The Worst twins were outstanding, and Christian High won the game 42-26.

"Well, gentlemen," Coach Coors mused as they made their way back to Grand Harbor, "it would appear we have our work cut out for us. Anyone have any suggestions how we can stop the Worst twins?"

"Induct them into the army before Friday," was Dutchie's suggestion, which was just a practical as

Bergie's: "Break their thumbs."

"Anyone else?" Coach Coors wanted to know, hoping Woody would come up with a real idea.

"I wonder," Woody began. "I wonder if they are more than twice as good together as they are separate." There was a thoughtful silence before he continued. "I think the George twin is the better player. I don't think Joel can dribble with his left hand and he doesn't move well to his left. If we can set up a defense that traps Joel, we can force him to the right. I believe that will handicap him, and if we can drive on him and force him to his left on defense, maybe we can get him to foul out. Then we'll see if George is as good without Joel."

That started a discussion that lasted all the way to Grand Harbor.

*****

"This is the same Grand Rapids Christian team that we narrowly beat for the second win of the season," Coach Coors lectured his team before the start of the next practice. "They also only have one loss—to us—so you can be sure they will be looking for revenge. You may recall they are a small team, and very fast.

"They have two outstanding guards: the Worst twins, George and Joel. It's said they have a sixth sense about where the other is and don't have to look to find each other. Several of us went to see them play last evening, and the sixth sense thing is no exaggeration.

"You probably remember that we beat them by changing our game strategy and shooting from the perimeter. We're going to modify that strategy a bit, and I've brought this blackboard to the gym to show you what I have in mind.

"We're going to start with the premise that Joel Worst is the worst of the Worsts. Don't get any ideas, here. You can be worse than Joel Worst and still be very, very good. But here's what we're going to try to do . . . ."

*****

During practice Woody took the role of Joel Worst, dribbling only with his right hand. Coach Coors taught Scooter how to force him to the right side of the offensive court, where Scooter and Dutchie tried to double team him and force an error. And Woody made plenty. Marv Peters, who would likely be playing opposite Joel on offense, practiced driving to the basket and forcing Joel left, hoping to make him foul. Together the team planned to shut down Joel and thus minimize the effectiveness of George.

*****

After practice that night, Woody was exhausted.

"Hi mom. Heard from Uncle Lou?"

"No, honey, no word." Then she turned and looked at him. "What happened to you? You look all tuckered out!"

"I tried to be somebody I'm not."

"Dear me, put your things down and tell me about it."

"I tried to be Joel Worst, and at my best, I'm not as good as Joel Worst is at his worst."

"Well, as my father used to say, 'Good, better, best. Do good on your better until your better's best.' As I recall, he didn't have a saying about your worst. Well, anyway, you have just enough time to read the paper before dinner."

Woody headed to the living room, where he spread the paper out on the floor and stretched out to read it.

This time the story was on page six:

1300 Half-Starved, Ill-Clothed Prisoners Liberated at Bilibid

BILIBID PRISON, Manila, P.I. Musty, filthy old Bilibid, erstwhile Japanese prison of horrors, was a begrimed citadel of American freedom today. The 37th Division infantry opened its doors Sunday for the liberation of its half-starved, ill-clothed prisoners of war.

Old Bilibid was in such a deplorable condition that the ancient Spanish prison had been abandoned

> by the Filipino government before the war. But the Japanese made full use of its torture chambers.
>
> Many of the inmates were too weak to walk and the others were described by their liberators as being little more than walking skeletons having survived on under 8 ounces of food per day.
>
> In describing the horrific treatment received at the hands of their Japanese captors, one of the survivors was quoted as saying, "The ones that died early on were the lucky ones."

Woody shivered as he read the account and tried to imagine existing on less than one cup of food a day. From the description in the newspaper, hundreds of prisoners had died, and the survivers were suffering from malnutrition, beriberi, dysentery—their bodies were a mess. He wondered about their minds after three years of this kind of torture. He knew his mother prayed desperately that her brother was alive. But if he was, who would he be? What had he become? "Be careful what you pray for," Woody said to himself.

On Thursday night the *Tribune* carried another headline that brought some more hope to the Nelson household:

2,146 Are Rescued from Fourth Jap Prison Camp

PARATROOPERS, SEA, LAND UNITS SUPRISE CAMP

MANILA, P.I. Striking with quick precision yesterday from the sky, by land, and by water, American troops and Filipino guerrillas brought relief and freedom to 2,146 Allied captives in an internment camp at Los Banos, 30 miles south of Manila.

Yesterday's dramatic raid brought the total of men, women and children rescued this month to approximately 7,700. . . .

A picture accompanied the story showing two men liberated from the Santo Tomas prison camp. Their skin hung loosely over their bones. One man's weight had dropped from 178 to 102 pounds.

Mrs. Nelson read and re-read the story as if she might find her brother's name between the lines. "Do you suppose he hasn't called because he didn't make it?" she asked no one in particular.

"I haven't read or heard of anyone being notified one way or the other," Mr. Nelson tried to reassure his wife.

"I don't think we have very much longer to wait, Mom," Woody said, trying to hide his fear that they hadn't heard because there was no one to make the call.

"I suppose not. I suppose not," was all she could think to reply.

Chapter 17

A Necessary Circus Stunt

The locker room was unusually quiet as the Pirates dressed for the game against Grand Rapids Christian. There was talk in the papers that the eventual Class B champion might be decided with this game.

Scooter tried to lighten the mood. "Woody, what's the Question of the Day?"

"You mean besides 'Are we gonna win tonight?'"

"Hey!" Doolie warned. "Let's not be having any questions about that. Of course we're gonna' win! Right, men?"

"Right!" came the chorus.

"Okay, okay," said Woody. "You want the Woodrow Peabody Nelson Question of the Day?"

"Let's hear it."

"If you try to fail and succeed, which have you done?"

Some heavy philosophical discussion followed. Several thought you had succeeded, while others argued that you could not succeed if you failed. Finally Jake turned the question back to Woody.

"Okay, Woody, what's the answer? If you try to fail and you succeed, have you succeeded or failed?"

"I have no idea. I only have the Question of the Day. I don't profess to have the Answer of the Day. But one way to look at it is if you try to succeed and you fail, you've failed. The opposite of failure is success. I'd say that to try to fail and succeeding is the opposite of trying to succeed and failing. If the opposite of failure is success, you must have succeeded if you tried to fail and succeeded."

There was silence in the locker room until Doolie slowly leaned toward Dutchie and whispered loudly so everyone could hear, "What'd he say?"

The door of the locker room opened and Coach Coors entered. "It's almost time for warm-ups, gentlemen. Every Pirate who takes the floor tonight will have to dig deep, draw on all his resources, and play the best game of his life if we expect to win. Let's stick to our game plan and execute well. And let's represent ourselves, our families, and our school the best we know how. Good luck and let's go!"

*****

The game was like a giant chess match with each coach trying this strategy and that. Woody's assessment was correct. Joel Worst couldn't dribble with his left hand or move well to his left. His brother, George, was the better player, and tonight he was unstoppable. Bergie was having a great night as well. If a Pirate missed a shot, Bergie was all over the rebound, making put back after put back.

Offenses and defenses were tried and abandoned. The Pirates took shots from the perimeter and took an early lead until the Eagles started to challenge them. Then the Pirates worked the ball down low for the high percentage shots. Each time Joel Worst came out to challenge Scooter, Scooter drove to the basket, and Joel fouled him enough so that the twins switched and George guarded Scooter. When the buzzer signaled the end of the first half, Grand Harbor held a very slim 21-20 lead. Joel Worst had turned the ball over five times and had accumulated four fouls. One more and he would be out. George, on the other hand, had no fouls and had scored 13 points.

*****

"Well, gentlemen," said Coach Coors in the locker room, "we've almost got the one twin to foul out. Mr. Peters, I want you to drive on him every chance you get. If you commit a foul or two, so be it. But let's try to get him out of the game as early as we can."

The second half was a nail biter. Marv Peters drove on Joel Worst on the first possession. The twin tried not to guard too closely for fear of fouling out, but in getting out of Marv's way, he ran smack into Doolie, who wasn't afraid to embellish the collision. The Eagle was called for charging, and his fifth foul forced him to leave the game.

There were sighs of anguish from the Christian fans and smug smiles of satisfaction from Grand Harbor's fans. The twin's absence didn't have the desired effect, however. The other twin, George, went on a rampage. It seemed everything he threw toward the basket went in. With two minutes to go, and after the lead had changed hands several times, the score was tied. Marv and Scooter had four fouls each from trying to stop an unstoppable George Worst. The Christian coach called time out. As the cheerleaders took to the court, the players trotted to their respective benches.

"Everyone in the huddle," Coach Coors commanded. "What we've been doing has kept us in the game thus far. I want you to continue with the flexible offense. If they collapse to prevent us from working the ball in close, shoot from the perimeter and get the rebounds. If they come out to challenge the perimeter shots, work the ball in for the high percentage shots. Secory and Peters, don't be afraid to be aggressive with the Worst boy. I know you have four fouls, but if he smells that you're afraid to guard him, he'll have your bacon before breakfast. Okay, play smart. If we lose, there's no tomorrow!"

Christian took the ball out and worked it about before George Worst drove in on Scooter and drew a foul. That meant Scooter had fouled out.

"Jacob Merrill. Report in for Secory," Coach Coors directed. He patted Jake on the pants as he went by and handed Scooter a towel as he came off the floor. "Well done against a worthy opponent, Secory. You've nothing to be ashamed of."

The Worst boy made the first free throw and the Christian fans rose to their feet with a roar. But he missed the second, and Dutchie came down with the rebound to the noisy delight of the Pirate fans. Christian set up defensively at the other end of the court, giving the Pirate players the perimeter shot. After several passes, Jake sank a 25-foot shot, and the Pirate fans thundered their approval. Grand Harbor 39, Grand Rapids Christian 38.

On the next two possessions, both teams turned the ball over while precious time ticked away. A Christian player walked with the ball, and Doolie missed catching a bullet pass from Marv that could have resulted in an easy lay-up. When Christian took the ball down the court, George Worst missed a long two-handed set shot and Bergie got the rebound. But when the Pirates brought the ball down, Worst slapped away a pass from Jake and raced down the court for an easy lay-up. With 15 seconds to go, Coach Coors called for a time out.

"Listen up, men." He diagrammed a play on a small chalk board. "We want to get the ball into the hands of our best shooter—that's you, Nagtzaam. But it's important that you shoot soon enough so that there is a chance for a rebound and a put back. The rebound is essential if he misses. So Greenberg and Higgins, that rebound is your responsibility. Don't forget, Merrill, you only have three seconds to get the ball inbounds. Let's go!"

When Woody sat down, he crossed all the fingers on both hands and then crossed his thumbs. The crowd became so quiet that you could hear the squeaks of the gym shoes as the players stopped and wheeled. You could also hear the sound of the leather slapping into Marv's hands when Jake managed to get the in-bound pass to him. Marv dribbled the ball and waited for Jake to get into position. With ten seconds on the clock, Jake set up and the pass came to him as planned. He faked a pass to Doolie, Bergie stepped in front of the man guarding Dutchie, and Dutchie moved into the clear. Jake almost made the pass to Dutchie, but suddenly glimpsed George Worst moving in to intercept the pass. Jake held on. With five seconds to go he had an Eagle all over him and he wasn't facing the basket. All he could hear was "Shoot! Shoot!" ringing in his ears. Jake didn't have a good hook shot and he knew it. He whipped a pass over to Marv, who didn't hesitate. His two-handed set shot arced toward the basket, but it made the clanging sound Coach Coors hated. "Clang is the harshest, most disappointing sound I know. It's the sound of a missed opportunity, a failed attempt."

Now Bergie, who had timed his jump as if there was going to be a rebound, was controlling the ball at the top of its bounce off the rim. Woody didn't need to look at the clock to know there wasn't enough time for Bergie to come down with the rebound and put the ball back up into the basket for an easy lay-up. They would lose by one point.

But as Woody and every eye in the gym watched, Bergie didn't come down with the ball. Instead he held the ball over the basket and sent it crashing straight down through the hoop as the buzzer sounded. He had slammed it down though the basket. **HE HAD SLAM DUNKED THE BASKETBALL!**

Woody came off his chair like a rocket! Bergie had won the game on a slam dunk when slam dunks were not allowed! Woody was about to join the rest of his teammates who were piling on Bergie, when he looked back at Coach Coors. The coach's eyes met Woody's and his clenched jaw relaxed into a grin. "Circus stunt!" he yelled to no one in particular and then jogged over to shake the hand of the disappointed Eagles coach.

*****

"I'm so sorry you didn't get to play tonight, honey," Woody's mother said when he climbed into the car. "It's nice that the team won, but I know how disappointed you must be not to have played even once."

Woody looked at Scooter, who was riding home with the Nelsons. Scooter was smiling.

"Mrs. Nelson," Scooter replied. "Woody won the game for us."

"What? He didn't play a lick. Not once. How can you say he won the game for you?" Mr. Nelson turned away from the road to ask.

"I'd like to hear that, too," Woody's mother turned in her seat to look at Scooter.

"Well, first of all, he figured out that the one Worst twin didn't move to his left very well. That allowed us to plan an offense that got him to foul out early in the game. Second, Woody figured out that that kid couldn't dribble with his left hand, which allowed us to set up a defense that made him turn the ball over several times—five, I think. But most importantly, Woody invented the shot that Bergie won the game with."

"Really? Is that true, honey?"

"Well, Coach Coors didn't put me on the team because I'm six foot six or because I can sink two-handed set shots from 25 feet. He put me on the team to help with strategy."

"We're all glad of that, little buddy," Scooter nudged him with his elbow.

Suddenly Woody realized something. He turned to Scooter. "That wasn't the first time Bergie ever tried that shot. That was too graceful, too controlled."

Scooter smiled broadly. "Bergie and I have been working on jamming the ball through the hoop in my driveway ever since you taught us to do it. He's real good at it. Almost poetry in motion. But I can do it, too, if the weather's just right."

"Well, I'll be jiggered," Woody replied.

*****

When the Nelsons got home, Woody could hear the phone ringing through the back door and he raced in to answer it.

"Who could be calling us at this hour?" his mother asked with a worried tone.

"'Calls in the night will give you a fright' is what the Widow Bach always says," returned her husband, who was still too happy about his son's accomplishments to worry.

"Hello?" Woody said breathlessly when he got to the phone.

"This is the overseas operator. I have a person-to-person call for . . ." the operator hesitated for a moment, "for a Mrs., uh, Sweetcakes Nelson."

Oh, my God! He made it, Woody thought as he said, "One moment, please" into the telephone mouthpiece.

"Mom, it's for you," he said as nonchalantly as he could. He didn't want to spoil the wonderful surprise she was about to get.

"Who is it?" she whispered with her hand over the mouthpiece.

"It's a woman. I didn't recognize her voice," Woody replied.

Epilogue

We'd like you to know that if we reprinted a story from the newspaper or related a story from the newspaper, that story actually appeared in the *Grand Haven Tribune* in substance as we reported it in this book. We used the names of those soldiers who were reported as missing in action, wounded in action, or killed in action to honor their service and their sacrifice to our country and our freedoms. We do confess, however, to some literary license with dates to suit the purpose of our story.

We'd also like you to know something about the characters in our book who are based on real people:

General Dwight D. Eisenhower became the 34th president of the United States.

General George S. Patton died on December 20, 1945, as the result of injuries sustained when he was thrown out of a jeep.

Richard "Uncle Rich" Nagtzaam survived the war and came home to his wife, Winifred. He won the Bronze Star for Valor. Many of the stories he writes home about are his own. Some of the stories were told to us by other veterans, including Harvey Bylsma, Henry Swartz, Wally Roach, and Joseph Hettinga. The book is the richer for their input.

Donald "Dutchie" Nagtzaam married Lois "Webb" Webber and enlisted in the Army Air Corps. He became a bombardier instructor, but never went overseas.

Johanna Boven lived to be 92 years old and her ability to recite long passages of poetry and the Bible never diminished. Her son, Robert, survived the war and wrote a fascinating book entitled *Most Decorated Soldier in WWII: Matt Urban*. The story about Robert and his mother is just as they told it to us. We, like the people in our story, believe Johanna Boven.

E. V. Cohrs was a teacher at Grand Haven High School and as a basketball coach led his teams to many victorious seasons, including state championships. The story of the Leyden jar is true, but it happened in Jay's physics class to Wesley Vryhof, who was both a physics teacher and a basketball coach at Grand Rapids Christian High School.

Miss Nettie Abrams was Jay's junior high school world history teacher at Southwest Christian School in Grand Rapids, Michigan. She is deceased.

The entire story about the Greenbergs and Isaac Greenberg's parents is fiction. Unfortunately, what happened to many Jews in Europe during the time the Nazis were in power wasn't fiction, and our story carries no exaggerations.

The Worst twins, Joel and George, were great athletes and did play basketball for the Grand Rapids Christian Eagles. They are both deceased.

Special mention goes to Marvin Peter Bylsma, our uncle and great-uncle as well as being a great uncle. He was an outstanding basketball player at the high school and collegiate level and witnessed the invention of the slam dunk. He will be upset that in our story, he misses the last shot of the final game, because he would have us believe he never missed a basket or a meal.

There are others whose names or personas we borrowed, and we would like to thank them. Carl "Bub" Denten, Kasey "Casey" Bylsma, Jacob Merrill Bylsma, David Berilla, Gertude "Widow Bach" Baak (deceased), and Eugene Westerhof, as well as other students of Grand Haven High School class of 1944.

And yes, there was a rifle club as we described it.

About the Authors

Dan Bylsma is a professional hockey player (assistant captain of the Mighty Ducks of Anaheim, 2002-2003) who loves a variety of sports beyond his profession. When he is not on the ice, Dan writes a hockey newsletter, runs a summer hockey camp, and speaks to kids and parents about good sportsmanship and keeping games fun. Dan and his wife Mary Beth live with their son in Los, Angeles, California and Grand Haven, Michigan.

Jay M. Bylsma and his wife Nancy have spent much of their lives at athletic events of their children, four sons and one daughter. Mr. Bylsma is a financial consultant with a keen interest in sports, music, and writing. He and Dan have written two hockey books, *So Your Son Wants to Play in the NHL* and *So You Want to Play in the NHL*and a novel for young readers, *Pitcher's Hands is OUT!*